FIVE HAVE PLENTY OF FUN

Five Have Plenty Of Fun

Enid Blyton

Hodder
Children's
Books

a division of Hodder Headline plc

First published in Great Britain in 1954
by Hodder and Stoughton

This edition 1991

10 9 8 7

A Catalogue record for this book is available from the
British Library

ISBN 0-340-54888-6

Printed and bound in Great Britain
by Cox & Wyman Ltd, Reading, Berks

Hodder Children's Books
A Division of Hodder Headline plc
338 Euston Road
London NW1 3BH

Contents

1 At Kirrin Cottage

'I feel as if we've been at Kirrin for about a month already!' said Anne, stretching herself out on the warm sand, and digging her toes in. 'And we've only just come!'

'Yes – it's funny how we settle down at Kirrin so quickly,' said Dick. 'We only came yesterday, and I agree with you, Anne – it seems as if we've been here ages. I love Kirrin.'

'I hope this weather lasts out the three weeks we've got left of the holiday,' said Julian, rolling away from Timmy, who was pawing at him, trying to make him play. 'Go away, Timmy. You're too energetic. We've bathed, had a run, played ball – and that's quite enough for a little while. Go and play with the crabs!'

'Woof!' said Timmy, disgusted. Then he pricked up his ears as he heard a tinkling noise from the promenade. He barked again.

'Trust old Timmy to hear the ice-cream man,' said Dick. 'Anyone want an ice-cream?'

Everyone did, so Anne collected the money and went off to get the ice-creams, Timmy close at her heels. She came back with five cartons of ice-cream, Timmy jumping up at her all the way.

'I can't think of anything nicer than lying down on hot sand with the sun on every part of my body, eating an ice-cream, and knowing there are still three weeks' holiday in front of us – at Kirrin too!' said Dick.

'Yes. It's heaven,' said Anne. 'It's a pity your father

has visitors today, George. Who are they? Have we got to dress up for them?'

'I don't think so,' said George. 'Timmy, you've eaten your ice-cream in one gulp. What a frightful waste!'

'When are these people coming?' asked Dick.

'About half past twelve,' said George. 'They're coming to lunch – but thank goodness Father told Mother he didn't want a pack of children gobbling all round him and his friends at lunch, so Mother said we could go in at half past twelve, say how-do-you-do and then clear off again with a picnic basket.'

'I must say I think your father has some good ideas at times,' said Dick. 'I suppose they are some scientist friends of his?'

'Yes. Father's working on some great scheme with these two men,' said George. 'One of them's a genius, apparently, and has hit on an idea that's too wonderful for words.'

'What kind of modern idea is it?' said Julian, lazily, holding out his fingertips for Timmy to lick off smears of ice-cream. 'Some spaceship to take us on day trips to the moon – or some new bomb to set off – or . . .'

'No, I *think* it's something that will give us heat, light and power for almost nothing!' said George. 'I heard Father say that it's the simplest and best idea anyone had ever worked out, and he's awfully excited about it. He called it a "gift to mankind" and said he was proud to have anything to do with it.'

'Uncle Quentin is very clever, isn't he?' said Anne. George's father was the uncle of Julian, Dick and Anne, and they were cousins to George – short for Georgina. Once more they had all come down to Kirrin for part of their holiday, the last three weeks.

George's father was certainly clever. All the same, George sometimes wished that he was a more *ordinary* parent, one who would play cricket or tennis with children, and not be so horrified at shouting and laughter and silly jokes. He always made a fuss when George's mother insisted that George should have her cousins to stay.

'Noisy, rowdy, yelling kids!' he said. 'I shall lock myself in my study and stay there!'

'All right, dear,' said his wife. 'You do that. But you know perfectly well that they will be out practically all day long. George *must* have other children to stay sometimes, and her three cousins are the nicest ones I know. George loves having them here.'

The four cousins were very careful not to upset George's father. He had a very hot temper and shouted at the top of his voice when he was angry. Still, as Julian said, he really couldn't *help* being a genius, and geniuses weren't ordinary people.

'Especially *scientific* geniuses who might easily blow up the whole world in a fit of temper,' said Julian, solemnly.

'Well, I wish he wouldn't keep blowing *me* up if I let a door bang, or set Timmy barking,' said George.

'That's only to keep his hand in,' said Dick. 'Just a bit of practice at blowing up!'

'Don't be an ass,' said George. 'Does anyone feel like another bathe?'

'No. But I don't mind going and lying in the very edge of the sea, and letting the waves there just curl over me,' said Dick. 'I'm absolutely baked lying here.'

'It *sounds* lovely,' said Anne. 'But the hotter you are the colder the water feels.'

'Come on!' said Dick, getting up. 'I shall hang my tongue out and pant like Timmy soon.'

They all went down to the edge of the water and lay down flat in the tiny curling waves there. Anne gave a little shriek.

'It feels icy! I knew it would. I can't lie down in it yet – I can only sit up!'

However they were soon all lying full-length in the shallow waves at the edge of the sea, sliding down the sand a little every now and again as the tide ebbed farther from them. It was lovely to feel the cool fingers of the sea on every part of them.

Suddenly Timmy barked. He was not in the water with them, but was just at the edge. He thought that lying down in the sea was quite unnecessary! George raised her head.

'What's the matter?' she said. 'There's nobody coming.'

But Dick had heard something too. He sat up hurriedly. 'Gosh, I believe that's someone ringing a bell for us. It sounds like the bell from Kirrin Cottage!'

'But it *can't* be dinner-time yet!' said Anne in dismay.

'It must be,' said Julian, leaping up. 'Blow! This is what comes of leaving my watch in my anorak pocket! I ought to have remembered that time at Kirrin goes more quickly than anywhere else!'

He ran up the beach to his anorak and took his wristwatch from the pocket. 'It's one o'clock!' he yelled. 'In fact, it's a minute past. Buck up, we'll be awfully late!'

'Blow!' said George. 'Mother won't be at all pleased with us, because those two scientist people will be there!'

They collected their anoraks and tore up the beach. It was not very far to Kirrin Cottage, fortunately, and they were soon running in at the front gate. There was a very large car outside, one of the latest American models. But there was no time to examine it!

They trailed in quietly at the garden door. George's mother met them, looking rather cross.

'Sorry, Aunt Fanny,' said Julian. 'Please forgive us. It was my fault entirely. I'm the only one with a watch.'

'Are we *awfully* late?' asked Anne. 'Have you begun lunch yet? Would you like us just to take our picnic basket and slip off without interrupting?'

'No,' said her aunt. 'Fortunately your uncle is still shut up in his study with his friends. I've sounded the gong once but I don't expect they've even *heard* it! I rang the bell for you because I thought that any moment they might come out, and your uncle would be cross if you weren't there just to say how-do-you-do!'

'But Father's friends don't *usually* want to see us,' said George, surprised.

'Well, one of them has a girl a bit younger than you, George – younger than Anne too, I think,' said her mother. 'And he specially asked to see you all, because his daughter is going to your school next term.'

'We'd better buck up and have a bit of a wash then,' said Julian – but at that very moment the study door opened, and his Uncle Quentin came out with two men.

'Hallo – are these your kids?' said one of the men, stopping.

'They've just come in from the beach,' said Aunt Fancy hurriedly. 'I'm afraid they are not really fit to be seen. I . . .'

'Great snakes!' said the man. 'Don't you dare to apologise for kids like these! I never saw such a fine lot in my life – they're wunnerful!'

He spoke with an American accent, and beamed all over his face. The children warmed to him at once. He turned to George's father. 'These all yours?' he asked. 'I bet you're proud of them! How did they get that tan

– they're so dark! My, my – wish my Berta looked like that!'

'They're not all mine,' said Uncle Quentin, looking quite horrified at the thought. 'Only this one is mine,' and he put his hand on George's shoulder. 'The others are nephews and a niece.'

'Well, I must say you've got a fine boy,' said the American, ruffling George's short curls. As a rule she hated people who did that, but because he mistook her for a boy, she grinned happily!

'My girl's going to your school,' he said to Anne. 'Give her a bit of help, will you? She'll be scared stiff at first.'

'Of course I will,' said Anne, taking a liking to the huge loud-voiced American. He didn't look a bit like a scientist. The other man did, though. He was round-shouldered and wore owl-like glasses, and, as Uncle Quentin often did, he stared into the distance as if he was not hearing a single word that anyone said.

Uncle Quentin thought this gossiping had lasted long enough. He waved the children away.

'Come and have lunch,' he said to the other men. The second man followed him at once, but the big American stayed behind. He thrust his hand into his pocket and brought out a pound coin. He gave it to Anne.

'Spend that on yourselves,' he said. 'And be kind to my Berta, won't you?'

He disappeared into the dining-room and shut the door with a loud bang. 'Goodness – what will Father say to a bang like *that*!' said George, with a sudden giggle. 'I like him, don't you? That must be *his* car outside. I can't imagine the other man even riding a bicycle, let alone driving a car!'

'Children – take your picnic basket and *go*!' said

Aunt Fanny, urgently. 'I *must* run and see that everything is all right!'

She thrust a big basket into Julian's hands, and
disappeared into the dining-room. Julian grinned as he
felt the weight of the basket.

'Come along,' he said. 'This feels good! Back to the
beach, everyone!'

2 A visitor in the night

The Five were on the beach in two minutes, and Julian undid the basket. It was full of neatly packed sandwiches, and packets of biscuits and chocolate. A bag contained ripe plums, and there were two bottles of lemonade.

'Home-made!' said Dick, taking it out. 'And icy-cold. And what's this? A fruit cake – a *whole* fruit cake – we're in luck.'

'Woof,' said Timmy, approvingly, and sniffed inside the basket.

Wrapped in brown paper were some biscuits and a bone, together with a small pot of paste. George undid the packet. '*I* packed these for you, Timmy,' she said. 'Say thank you!'

Timmy licked her so lavishly that she cried out for mercy. 'Pass me the towel, Ju!' she said. 'Timmy's made my face all wet. Get away now, Timmy – you've thanked me quite enough! Get *away*, I said. How can I spread paste on your biscuits if you stick your nose into the pot all the time?'

'You spoil Timmy dreadfully,' said Anne. 'All right, all right – you needn't scowl at me, George! I agree that he's *worth* spoiling. Take your bone a *bit* farther away from me, Tim – it's smelly!'

They were soon eating sardine sandwiches with tomatoes, and egg-and-lettuce sandwiches after that. Then they started on the fruit cake and the lemonade.

'I can't think why people ever have table-meals when they can have picnics,' said Dick. 'Think of Uncle and Aunt and those two men tucking into a hot meal indoors on a day like this. Phew!'

'I liked that big American,' said George.

'Aha! We all know why,' said Dick, annoyingly. 'He thought you were a boy. Will you ever grow out of that, George?'

'Timmy's trying to get at the cake!' said Anne. 'Quick, George, stop him!'

They all lay back on the sand after their picnic, and Julian began a long story of some trick that he and Dick had played on their form-master at school. He was most annoyed because nobody laughed at the funny part, and sat up to see why.

'All asleep!' he said, in disgust. Then he cocked his head just as Timmy pricked up his ears. A loud roaring noise came to him.

'Just the American revving up his car, do you think, Tim?' said Julian. The boy stood up and saw the great car tearing down the sea road.

The day was too hot to do anything but laze. The Five were quite content to do that on their first day together again. Soon they would want to plan all kinds of things, but the first day at Kirrin was a day for picking up old threads, teasing Timmy, getting into the 'feel' of things again, as Dick said.

Dick and Julian had been abroad for four weeks, and Anne had been away to camp and had had a school friend to stay with her at home afterwards. George had been alone at Kirrin so it was wonderful to all the Five to meet together once more for three whole summer weeks. At Kirrin too, Kirrin by the sea, with its lovely beach, its fine boating – and its exciting little island across Kirrin Bay!

As usual the first day or two passed in a kind of

dream, and then the children began to plan exciting things to do.

'We'll go to Kirrin Island again,' said Dick. 'We haven't been there for ages.'

'We'll go fishing in Lobster Cove,' said Julian.

'We'll go and explore some of the caves in the cliffs,' said George. 'I meant to do that these hols, but somehow it's no fun going alone.'

On the third day, just as they were finishing making their beds, the telephone rang.

'I'll go!' yelled Julian to his aunt, and went to answer it. An urgent voice spoke at the other end.

'Who's that? Oh, you, Julian – you're Quentin's nephew, aren't you? Listen, tell your uncle I'm coming over tonight – yes, tonight. Latish, say. Tell him to wait up for me. It's important.'

'But, won't you speak to him yourself?' said Julian, surprised. 'I'll fetch him, if you'll . . .'

But the line had gone dead. Julian was puzzled. The man hadn't even given his name – but Julian had recognised the voice. It was the big, cheery American who had come to see his uncle two days before! What had happened? What was all the excitement about?

He went to find his uncle but he was not in his study. So he found his aunt instead.

'Aunt Fanny,' he said, 'I *think* that was the big American on the phone – the one who came to lunch the other day. He said I was to tell Uncle Quentin that he was coming here tonight – late, he said – and that Uncle was to wait up for him, because it was important.'

'Dear me!' said his aunt, startled. 'Is he going to stay the night then? We've no bedroom free now you and the others are here.'

'He didn't say, Aunt Fanny,' said Julian. 'I'm awfully sorry not to be able to tell you any details – but just as I was saying I'd fetch Uncle Quentin, he rang off – in the very middle of what I was saying.'

'How mysterious!' said his aunt. 'And how annoying. *How* can I put him up, if he wants to stay? I suppose he'll come roaring down at midnight in that enormous car of his. I only hope nothing's gone wrong with this latest work your uncle is doing. I know it's tremendously important.'

'Perhaps Uncle will know the American's telephone number and he can ring him up to find out a bit more,' said Julian, helpfully. 'Where is Uncle?'

'He's gone down to the post-office, I think,' said his aunt. 'I'll tell him when he gets back.'

Julian told the others about the mysterious phone call. Dick was pleased.

'I didn't have a chance of getting a good look at that enormous car the other day,' he said. 'I think I'll keep awake tonight till the American comes and then nip down and have a look at it. I bet it's got more gadgets on the dashboard than any car I've ever seen!'

Uncle Quentin appeared to be as surprised as anyone else at the phone call, and was inclined to blame Julian for not finding out more details.

'What's he want now?' he demanded, almost as if Julian ought to know! 'I fixed everything up with him the other day. *Every*thing! Each of us three has his own part to do. Mine's the least important, as it happens – and his is the most important. He took all the papers away with him; he can't have left any behind. Coming down in the middle of the night like this – quite extraordinary!'

None of the children except Dick meant to stay awake and listen for the American's coming. Dick put on his bedside light and took up a book to read. He knew he would fall asleep and not wake up for any noise, if he didn't somehow keep himself wide awake!

He listened as he read, his ear alert to hear the coming of any car. Eleven o'clock came – then midnight struck. He listened to the twelve dongs from the big grandfather clock in the hall. Goodness – Uncle Quentin wouldn't be at all pleased that his visitor was so late!

He yawned, and turned over his page. He read on and on. Half past twelve. One o'clock. Then he thought he heard a sound downstairs and opened his door. Yes – it was Uncle Quentin in his study. Dick could hear his voice.

'Poor old Aunt Fanny must be up too,' he thought. 'I can hear their voices. Gosh, I shall soon fall asleep over my book. I'll slip down and out into the garden for a breath of fresh air. I shall keep awake then.'

He put on his dressing-gown and went quietly down the stairs. He undid the bolt of the garden door and slipped out. He stood listening for a moment, wondering if he would hear the roar of the American's car in the stillness of the night.

But all he heard was the sound of the tyres of a bicycle on the road outside. A bicycle! Who was riding about at this time of night? Perhaps it was the village policeman?

Dick stood in the shadows and watched. A man was on the bicycle. Dick could just make him out dimly, a big black shadow in the starlit night. To the boy's enormous surprise, he heard the sound of the man dismounting, then the swish of the leaves in the hedge as the bicycle was slung there.

Then someone came quietly up the path and went round to the window of the study. It was the only room in the house that was lit. Dick heard a tapping on the window, and then it was opened cautiously. His uncle's head appeared.

'Who is it?' he said, in a low tone. 'Is it you, Elbur?'

It apparently was. Dick saw that it was the big American who had visited his uncle two days before. 'I'll open the door,' said his aunt, but Elbur was already putting his leg across the window-sill!

Dick went back to bed, puzzled. How strange! Why should the American come so secretly in the night, why should he ride a bicycle instead of driving his car? He fell asleep still wondering.

He did not know whether the American rode away again, or whether his aunt made a bed for him on a couch downstairs. In fact, when he awoke the next morning, he really wondered if it had all been a dream.

He asked his aunt, when he went down to breakfast. 'Did that man who telephoned come last night?' he said.

His aunt nodded her head. 'Yes. But please say nothing about it. I don't want anyone to know. He's gone now.'

'Was it important?' asked Dick. 'Julian seemed to think it was, when he answered the phone.'

'Yes – it was important,' said Aunt Fanny. 'But not in the way you think. Don't ask me anything now, Dick. And keep out of your uncle's way. He's rather cross this morning.'

'Then something must have gone wrong with this new work he's doing,' thought Dick, and went to warn the others.

'It sounds rather exciting,' said Julian. 'I wonder what's up?'

They kept out of Uncle Quentin's way. They heard him grumbling loudly to his wife about something, they heard him slam down his desk-lid as he always did when he was bad-tempered, and then he settled down to his morning's work.

Anne came running to the others after a time, looking surprised. 'George! I've just been into our

'Whatever for?' said Julian, amazed.

'Because it so happens that her father knows more secrets about a new scheme we're planning than anyone else in the world,' said his uncle. 'And he says, quite frankly, that if this girl – what's her name now . . .'

'Berta,' said everyone, obligingly.

'That if this Berta is kidnapped, he will give away every single secret he knows to get her back,' said Uncle Quentin. 'Pah! What's he made of? Traitor to us all! How can he even *think* of giving away secrets for the sake of a silly girl?'

'Quentin, she's his only child and he adores her,' said Aunt Fanny. 'I should feel the same about George.'

'Women are always soft and silly,' said her husband, in a tone of great disgust. 'It's a good thing *you* don't know any secrets – you'd give them away to the milkman!'

This was so ridiculous that the children laughed. Uncle Quentin glared at them.

'This is no laughing matter. It has been a great shock to me to be told by one of the leading scientists of the world that he feels certain he might give all our secrets to the enemy if this – this . . .'

'Berta,' said everyone again, at once.

'If this Berta was kidnapped,' went on Uncle Quentin. 'So he came to ask if we'd take this – this Berta into our own home for three weeks. By that time the scheme will be finished and launched, and our secrets will be safe.'

There was a silence. Nobody looked very pleased. In fact, George looked furious. She burst out at last.

'So *that's* who the bed is for in our room! Mother, have we *got* to be squashed up with nowhere to move about the room, for three whole weeks? It's too bad.'

It apparently was. Dick saw that it was the big American who had visited his uncle two days before. 'I'll open the door,' said his aunt, but Elbur was already putting his leg across the window-sill!

Dick went back to bed, puzzled. How strange! Why should the American come so secretly in the night, why should he ride a bicycle instead of driving his car? He fell asleep still wondering.

He did not know whether the American rode away again, or whether his aunt made a bed for him on a couch downstairs. In fact, when he awoke the next morning, he really wondered if it had all been a dream.

He asked his aunt, when he went down to breakfast. 'Did that man who telephoned come last night?' he said.

His aunt nodded her head. 'Yes. But please say nothing about it. I don't want anyone to know. He's gone now.'

'Was it important?' asked Dick. 'Julian seemed to think it was, when he answered the phone.'

'Yes – it was important,' said Aunt Fanny. 'But not in the way you think. Don't ask me anything now, Dick. And keep out of your uncle's way. He's rather cross this morning.'

'Then something must have gone wrong with this new work he's doing,' thought Dick, and went to warn the others.

'It sounds rather exciting,' said Julian. 'I wonder what's up?'

They kept out of Uncle Quentin's way. They heard him grumbling loudly to his wife about something, they heard him slam down his desk-lid as he always did when he was bad-tempered, and then he settled down to his morning's work.

Anne came running to the others after a time, looking surprised. 'George! I've just been into our room and what do you think! Aunt Fanny's put a camp-bed over in the corner – a camp-bed made up with blankets and everything! It looks an awful squash with two other beds as well in the room – mine and yours!'

'Gosh – someone else is coming to stay then – a girl,' said Dick. 'Or a woman. Aha! I expect it's a governess engaged to look after you and Anne, George, to see that you behave like little ladies!'

'Don't be an idiot,' said George, surprised and cross at the news. 'I'm going to ask Mother what it's all about. I won't have anyone else in our room. I just will *not!*'

But just as she was marching off to tell her mother this, the study door downstairs opened and her father bellowed into the hall, calling his wife.

'Fanny! Tell the children I want them. Tell them to come to my study AT ONCE!'

'Gracious – he does sound cross. Whatever can we have done?' said Anne, scared.

3 Annoying news

The four children and Timmy trooped down the stairs together. George's mother was in the hall, just going to call them.

'Oh, there you are,' she said. 'Well, I suppose you heard that you're wanted in the study. I'm coming too. And listen – *please* don't make any more fuss than you can help. I've had quite enough fuss made by Quentin!'

This was very mysterious! What had Aunt Fanny to do with whatever trouble there was? Into the study went the Five, Timmy too, and saw Uncle Quentin standing on the hearthrug looking as black as thunder.

'Quentin, *I* could have told the children,' began his wife, but he silenced her with a scowl exactly like the one George sometimes put on.

'I've got something to say to you,' he began. 'You remember those two friends of mine – scientists working on a scheme with me – you remember the big American?'

'Yes,' said everyone.

'He gave us a whole pound,' said Anne.

Uncle Quentin took no notice of that remark. 'Well,' he said, 'he's got a daughter – let's see now – she's got some silly name . . .'

'Berta,' said his wife.

'Don't interrupt me,' said Uncle Quentin. 'Yes, Berta. Well, Elbur, her father, has been warned that she's going to be kidnapped.'

'Whatever for?' said Julian, amazed.

'Because it so happens that her father knows more secrets about a new scheme we're planning than anyone else in the world,' said his uncle. 'And he says, quite frankly, that if this girl – what's her name now . . .'

'Berta,' said everyone, obligingly.

'That if this Berta is kidnapped, he will give away every single secret he knows to get her back,' said Uncle Quentin. 'Pah! What's he made of? Traitor to us all! How can he even *think* of giving away secrets for the sake of a silly girl?'

'Quentin, she's his only child and he adores her,' said Aunt Fanny. 'I should feel the same about George.'

'Women are always soft and silly,' said her husband, in a tone of great disgust. 'It's a good thing *you* don't know any secrets – you'd give them away to the milkman!'

This was so ridiculous that the children laughed. Uncle Quentin glared at them.

'This is no laughing matter. It has been a great shock to me to be told by one of the leading scientists of the world that he feels certain he might give all our secrets to the enemy if this – this . . .'

'Berta,' said everyone again, at once.

'If this Berta was kidnapped,' went on Uncle Quentin. 'So he came to ask if we'd take this – this Berta into our own home for three weeks. By that time the scheme will be finished and launched, and our secrets will be safe.'

There was a silence. Nobody looked very pleased. In fact, George looked furious. She burst out at last.

'So *that's* who the bed is for in our room! Mother, have we *got* to be squashed up with nowhere to move about the room, for three whole weeks? It's too bad.'

'For once you and I agree, George,' said her father. 'But I'm afraid you'll have to put up with it. Elbur is in such a state about this kidnapping warning that he couldn't be reasoned with. In fact he threatened to tear up all his figures and diagrams and burn them, if I didn't agree to this. That would mean we couldn't get on with the scheme.'

'But why has she got to come *here*?' said George, fiercely. 'Why put her on to *us*? Hasn't she any relations or friends she can go to?'

'George, don't be so fierce,' said her mother. 'Apparently Berta has no mother, and has been everywhere with her father. They have no relations in this country – and no friends they can trust. He won't send her back to America because he has been warned by the police that she might be followed there – and at the moment he can't leave this country himself to go with her.'

'But why choose *us*?' said George again. 'He doesn't know a thing about us!'

'Well,' said her mother, with a small smile, 'he met you all the other day, you know – and he was apparently very struck with you – and especially with *you*, George, though I can't imagine why. He said he'd rather his Berta was with you four than with any other family in the world.'

She paused and looked at the four, a harassed expression on her face. Julian went over to her.

'Don't you worry!' he said. 'We'll look after Berta! I won't pretend I'm pleased at having a strange girl to join us these last three precious weeks – but I can see her father's point of view – he's scared for Berta, and he's scared he might find himself spilling the beans if anything happened to her! It might be the only way he could get her back.'

'To think of such a thing!' burst out Uncle Quentin.

'All the work of the last two years! The man must be mad!'

'Now Quentin, don't think any more about it,' said his wife. 'I'm glad to have the child here. I would hate George to be kidnapped, and I know exactly how he feels. You won't even notice she's here. One more will make no difference.'

'So you say,' grumbled her husband. 'Anyway, it's settled.'

'When is she coming?' asked Dick.

'Tonight. By boat,' said his uncle. 'We'll have to let Joanna the cook into the secret – but nobody else. That's understood, isn't it?'

'Of course,' said the four at once. Then Uncle Quentin sat down firmly at his desk, and the children went hurriedly out of the room, Aunt Fanny behind them, and Timmy pushing between their ankles.

'It's such a pity, and I'm so sorry,' said Aunt Fanny. 'But I do feel we can't do anything else.'

'I bet Timmy will hate her,' said George.

'Now don't you go and make things difficult, George, old thing,' said Julian. 'We're all agreed it can't be helped, so we might as well make the best of it.'

'I hate making the best of things,' said George, obstinately.

'Well,' said Dick, amiably, 'Julian and Anne and I could go back home and take Berta with us if you hate everything so much. I don't particularly want to stay here for three weeks if you're going to put on a Hate all the time.'

'All right, I won't,' said George. 'I'm only letting off steam. You know that.'

'I'm never sure, with you,' said Dick, with a grin. 'Well, look – let's not spoil this one day when we *will* be by ourselves!'

They all tried valiantly to have as good a time as possible, and went out in George's boat for a long row to Lobster Cove. They didn't do any fishing there, but bathed from the boat instead, in water as green and clear as in an open-air bath. Timmy didn't approve of bathing from boats. It was quite easy to jump out of the boat into the water – but he found it extremely difficult to jump in again!

Aunt Fanny had again packed them a wonderful lunch. 'An extra good one to make up for disappointment,' she said, smiling. Anne had given her a hug for that. Here they had all been making such a fuss about having someone extra – and Aunt Fanny had been the only one to feel a real kindness for a child in danger.

They had enough food for tea too, and did not get home until the evening. The sea was calm and blue, and the children could see almost to the bottom of the water, when they leaned over the side of the boat. The sky was the colour of harebells as they rowed into the bay and up to the beach.

'Will Berta be there yet, do you suppose?' said George, mentioning the girl for the first time since they had set out that morning.

'I shouldn't think so,' said Julian. 'Your father said she would be coming tonight – and I imagine that as she's coming by boat, it will be dark – so that she won't be seen.'

'I expect she'll be feeling very scared,' said Anne. 'It must be horrid to be sent away to a strange place, to strange people. I should hate it!'

They beached the boat and left it high and dry. Then they made their way to Kirrin Cottage. Aunt Fanny was pleased to see them.

'You *are* in nice time for supper,' she said. 'Though if you ate all I gave you today for your picnics, you'll surely find it difficult to eat very much supper.'

'Oh, I'm *terribly* hungry,' said Dick. He sniffed, holding his nose up in the air just as Timmy often did. 'I believe you've been making your special tomato soup, with real tomatoes, Aunt Fanny!'

'You're too good at guessing,' said his aunt with a laugh. 'It was meant to be a surprise! Now go and wash and make yourselves tidy.'

'Berta hasn't come yet, I suppose, has she?' asked Julian.

'No,' said his aunt. 'And we'll have to think of another name for her, Julian. It would never do to call her Berta now.'

Uncle Quentin didn't appear for supper. 'He is having his in the study by himself,' said Aunt Fanny.

There was a sigh of relief. Nobody had looked forward to seeing Uncle Quentin that night. It took him quite a long time to get over any annoyance!

'How sunburnt you all are!' said Aunt Fanny, looking round the table. 'George, your nose is beginning to peel.'

'I know,' said George. 'I wish it didn't. Anne's never does. Gosh, I'm sleepy!'

'Well, go to bed as soon as you've finished your supper,' said her mother.

'I'd like to. But what about this Berta?' said George. 'What time is she coming? It would be rather mean to be in bed when she arrives.'

'I've no idea what time she will come,' said her mother. 'But I shall wait up, of course. There's no need for anyone else to. I expect she'll be tired and scared, so I shall give her something to eat – some of the tomato soup, if you've left any! – and then pop her into bed. I expect she would be quite glad not to have to meet any of you tonight.'

'Well – *I* shall go to bed,' said Dick. 'I heard Mr Elbur arriving last night, Aunt Fanny, and it was pretty late, wasn't it? I can hardly keep my eyes open tonight.'

'Come on, then – let's all go up,' said Julian. 'We can read if we can't sleep. Goodnight, Aunt Fanny. Thank you for that lovely picnic food again!'

All the four went upstairs, Anne and Dick yawning loudly, and setting the others off too. Timmy padded behind them, quite glad that George was going to bed so early.

They were all asleep in ten minutes. The boys slept like logs and didn't stir at all. The girls fell fast asleep for about four hours – and then George was awakened by hearing Timmy growl. She sat up at once.

'What is it?' she said. 'Oh – is it Berta arriving, Tim? Let's keep quiet and see what she's like!'

After a minute Timmy growled again. George heard the sound of quiet footsteps on the stairs. Then the bedroom door was slid softly open, and two people stood in the light of the landing lamp. One was Aunt Fanny.

The other, of course, was Berta.

4 Berta

George sat up in bed and stared at Berta. She looked very peculiar indeed. For one thing she was so bundled up in coats and wraps that it was difficult to see if she was fat or thin, tall or short, and for another thing she was crying so bitterly that her face was all screwed up.

Anne didn't wake up. Timmy was so astonished that, like George, he simply sat and stared.

'Tell Timmy not to make a sound,' whispered George's mother, afraid that the dog might bark the house down, once he began.

George laid a warning hand on Timmy. Her mother gave Berta a little push farther into the room.

'She's been terribly seasick, poor child,' she told George. 'And she's scared and upset. I want her to get into bed as soon as possible.'

Berta was still sobbing, but the sobs grew quieter as she began to feel less sick. George's mother was so kind and sensible that she felt comforted.

'Let's take these things off,' she said to Berta. 'My word, you *are* bundled up! But if you came in an open motorboat I expect you needed them.'

'What am I to call you?' asked Berta, with one last sniff.

'You'd better call me Aunt Fanny, as the others do, I think,' said George's mother. 'I expect you know why you've come to stay with us for a while, don't you?'

'Yes,' said Berta. 'I didn't want to come. I wanted to

stay with my father. I'm not afraid of being kidnapped. I've got Sally to look after me.'

'Who's Sally, dear?' asked Aunt Fanny, taking a coat
or two off Berta.

'My dog,' said Berta. 'She's downstairs in the basket
I was carrying.'

George pricked up her ears at *that* bit of news! 'A
dog!' she said. 'We can't have a dog here. Mine would
never allow that. Would you, Timmy?'

Timmy gave a small wuff. He was watching this
night arrival with great interest. Who was she? He was
longing to get down from George's bed and go to sniff
at her, but George had her hand on his collar.

'Well, I've brought my dog, and I just reckon she'll
have to stay now,' said Berta. 'The boat's gone back.
Anyway, I wouldn't go anywhere without Sally. I
told my father that, and he said all right then, take her
with you! So I did.'

'Mother, tell her how fierce Timmy is and that he
would fight any other dog who came here,' said
George, urgently. 'I won't have anybody else's dog at
Kirrin Cottage.'

To George's annoyance her mother took not the
slightest notice. She went on helping Berta take off
scarves, thick socks and goodness knows what.
George wondered how anyone could possibly exist in
all those clothes on a warm summer's night.

At last Berta stood in a simple jersey and skirt, a
slim, pretty little girl with large blue eyes and wavy
golden hair. She shook back her hair and rubbed her
face with a hanky.

'Thank you,' she said. 'Can I get Sally my dog
now?'

'Not tonight,' said Aunt Fanny. 'You see, you are to
sleep in that little camp-bed over in the corner – and I
can't let you have your dog here too, because she and

Timmy might fight unless we introduce them to one another properly. And there is no time to bother about that tonight. Do you feel hungry now? Would you like some tomato soup and biscuits?'

'Yes, please. I do feel a bit hungry,' said Berta. 'I've been so sick on that awful bumpy boat that I don't expect there's anything left inside me at all!'

'Well, look – you unpack your little night-case, and have a wash in the bathroom if you want to, and then get into your pyjamas,' said Aunt Fanny. 'Then hop into bed and I'll bring you up some soup.'

But one look at the scowling George made her change her mind. Better not leave poor Berta with an angry George on her very first night!

'I think perhaps I won't get the soup myself,' she said. 'George, you go and get it, will you? It's warming up in the saucepan on the stove downstairs. You'll see the little soup-cup on the table, and some biscuits too.'

George got out of bed, still looking very mutinous. She watched Berta shake out a nightdress from her night-case and pursed up her lips.

'She doesn't even wear pyjamas!' she thought. 'What a ninny! And she's had the nerve to bring her own dog, too – spoilt little thing! I wonder where it is? I've a good mind to have a look at it when I'm downstairs.'

But her mother had an idea that George might do that and she went to the door after her. 'George!' she said, warningly, 'I don't want you to open the dog's basket downstairs. I'm not having any dog-fights tonight. I shall put him in Timmy's kennel outside before I go to bed.'

George said nothing but went on downstairs. The soup was just about to boil and she whipped it off the stove at once. She poured it into the little soup-cup, placed it on the saucer, and put some biscuits on the side.

She heard a small whimpering sound, and turned round. It came from a fairly large basket over in the corner. George was terribly tempted to go and undo it – but she knew perfectly well that if the new dog ran upstairs to find its mistress, Timmy would bark and wake everybody up! It wasn't worth risking.

She took up the soup. Berta was now in the camp-bed and looked very cosy. Anne was still sleeping peacefully, quite undisturbed by all that was going on. Timmy had taken the opportunity of jumping off George's bed and had gone to examine this new-comer. He sniffed her delicately, and Berta put out her hand and stroked his head.

'What lovely eyes he's got,' she said. 'But he's a mongrel, isn't he? A sort of mixture-dog.'

'Don't you say anything like that to George,' said Aunt Fanny. 'She adores Timmy. Now – do you feel better? I hope you'll be happy with us, Berta, dear – I am sure you didn't want to come – but your father was so worried. And it will be nice for you to get to know Anne and Georgina before you go to their school next term.'

'Oh – was that Georgina – the one you called George?' said Berta in surprise. 'I wasn't really sure if she was a boy or not. My father told me there were three boys here and one girl – and that's the girl, isn't it – in bed there?'

She pointed to Anne. Aunt Fanny nodded. 'Yes, that's Anne. Your father thought George was a boy, that's why he told you there were three boys and only one girl here, I suppose. The two boys are in the next room.'

'I don't like George very much,' said Berta. 'She doesn't want me here, does she – or my dog?'

'Oh, you'll find George great fun when you get to know her,' said Aunt Fanny. 'Here she comes now with your soup.'

George came in with the soup, and was not at all pleased to see Timmy standing by the camp-bed, being petted by Berta. She set the soup down sharply and pushed Timmy away.

'Thank you,' said Berta, and took the soup-cup eagerly into her hands. 'What *lovely* soup!' she said. George got into bed and turned over on her side. She knew she was behaving badly, but the thought of someone daring to bring another *dog* to live at Kirrin Cottage was more than she could bear.

Timmy leapt up to lie at her feet as usual. Berta looked at this with much approval.

'I'll have Sally on *my* feet tomorrow!' she said. 'That's an awfully good idea. Pops – that's my father – always let me have Sally in my room, but she had to be in her basket, not on my bed. Tomorrow night she can sleep on my feet, like Timmy does on George's.'

'She will not,' said George, in a fierce voice. 'No dog sleeps in my bedroom except Timmy.'

'Now don't talk any more,' said Aunt Fanny, hurriedly. 'We can settle everything tomorrow when you're not so tired. I'll look after Sally tonight for you, I promise. Lie down now and go to sleep. You look as if you're half-asleep already!'

Berta was suddenly overcome with sleep and flopped down into bed. Her eyes closed, but she managed to force them open and look up at George's mother.

'Goodnight, Aunt Fanny,' she said, sleepily. 'That's what I was to call you, wasn't it? Thank you for being so kind to me.'

She was asleep almost before she had finished speaking. Aunt Fanny took up the soup-cup and went to the door. 'Are you awake, George?' she said.

George lay absolutely still. She knew that her mother was not pleased with her. It would be better to pretend to be fast asleep!

'I am sure you are awake,' said her mother. 'And I hope you are ashamed of yourself. I shall expect you to make up for this silly behaviour in the morning. It is a pity to behave in such a childish manner!'

She went out of the room, closing the door softly. George put out her hand to Timmy. She *was* ashamed of herself, but she wasn't at all certain that she would behave better in the morning. That silly, soppy girl! Her dog would be as silly as herself, she was sure! And Timmy would simply *hate* having another dog in the house. He would probably growl and snarl to such a degree that Berta would be forced to send her dog away.

'And a good thing too,' murmured George, as Timmy licked her fingers lovingly. '*You* don't want another girl in the house or another dog either, do you, Timmy? Especially a girl like that!'

Aunt Fanny saw to Berta's dog, and put her safely into Timmy's kennel outside. It had a little door to it, which could be shut, so the dog was safe there, and would not be able to run out.

She went back into the house, cleared up Berta's belongings a little, for they had been thrown higgledy-piggledy into the room, and then turned out the light.

She went upstairs to bed. Her husband had slept soundly all through Berta's late arrival. He had been very sure that he would wake up and welcome the girl as well as his wife; but he hadn't even stirred!

Aunt Fanny was glad. It was much easier for her to deal with a seasick, frightened girl by herself. She climbed thankfully into bed and lay down with a sigh.

'Oh dear – I don't look forward to the morning!

What will happen then, with George in this mood, and two dogs to sort out? Berta seems a nice little thing. Well – perhaps they will all get on better than I think!'

Yes – things wouldn't be too easy in the morning. That was quite certain!

5   In the morning

George was the first to wake up in the morning. She at
once remembered the events of the night before and
looked across at Berta in the camp-bed. The girl was
asleep, her wavy golden hair spread over the pillow.
George leaned across Anne's bed and gave her a sharp
nudge.

Anne woke up at once and gazed sleepily at George.
'What's the matter, George? Is it time to get up?'

'Look over there,' whispered George, nodding her
head towards Berta. Anne turned over and looked.
Unlike George she liked the look of Berta. Her sleeping face was pleasant and open, and her mouth turned
up, not down. Anne couldn't bear people whose
mouths turned down.

'She looks all right,' whispered back Anne. George
frowned.

'She howled like anything when she came,' she told
Anne. 'She's a real baby. *And* she's brought a dog!'

'Goodness – Timmy won't like that,' said Anne,
startled. 'Where is it?'

'Down in Timmy's kennel,' said George, still whispering. 'I haven't seen it. It was in a closed basket last
night and I didn't dare open it in case it tore upstairs
and had a fight with Tim. But it can't be very big. I
expect it's a horrible Peke, or some silly little lap-
dog.'

'Pekes aren't horrible,' said Anne. 'They may be
small and have funny little pug-noses, but they're

awfully brave. Fancy having another dog! I can't *think* what Timmy will say!'

'It's a pity Berta isn't our kind,' said George. 'Look at her pale face – not a scrap of sun-tan! And she looks *weedy*, doesn't she? I'm sure she couldn't climb a tree or row a boat, or . . .'

'Sh! She's waking up,' said Anne warningly.

Berta yawned and stretched herself. Then she opened her eyes and looked round. At first she had no idea, where she was, and then she suddenly remembered. She sat up.

'Hallo!' said Anne, and smiled at her. 'You weren't there when I came to bed last night. I was surprised to see you this morning.'

Berta took an immediate liking to Anne. 'She's got kind eyes,' she thought. 'She's not like the other girl. I like this one!'

She smiled back at Anne. 'Yes – I came in the middle of the night,' she said. 'I came by motorboat and the sea was so bumpy that I was frightfully sick. My father didn't come with me but a friend of his did and he carried me from the boat to Kirrin Cottage. Even my legs felt seasick!'

'Bad luck!' said Anne. 'You didn't really enjoy the adventure then!'

'No. I can do without adventures!' said Berta. 'I'm not keen on them. Especially when Pops gets all excited and worried about me – he fusses round me like a hen, dear old Pops. I shall hate being away from him.'

George was listening to all this. Not keen on adventures! Well, a girl like that wouldn't be, of course!

'*I'm* not very keen on adventures either,' said Anne. 'We've had plenty. I prefer adventures when they're all over!'

George exploded. 'Anne! How *can* you talk like that! We've had some *smashing* adventures, and we've enjoyed every one of them. If you feel like that we'll leave you out of the next one.'

Anne laughed. 'You won't! An adventure comes up all of a sudden, like a wind blowing up in the sky, and we're all in it, whether we like it or not. And you know that I like sharing things with you. I say – isn't it time we got up?'

'Yes,' said George, looking at the clock on the mantelpiece. 'Unless Berta wants to have her breakfast in bed? I bet she always does at home.'

'No, I don't. I hate meals in bed,' said Berta. 'I'm going to get up.'

She leapt out of bed and went to the window. Immediately she saw the wide sweep of the bay, sparkling in the morning sun, as blue as cornflowers. The sea-sparkle was reflected into the bedroom, and made it very bright indeed.

'Oh! I *wondered* why our room was so full of brilliant light,' said Berta. 'Now I know! What a view! Oh, how lovely the sea looks this morning! And what's that little island out there? What a lovely place it looks.'

'That's Kirrin Island,' said George, proudly. 'It belongs to *me*.'

Berta laughed, thinking that George was joking. 'Belongs to *you*! I bet you wish it did. It's really wunnerful!'

'*Wunnerful!*' said George imitating her. 'Can't you say "wonderful"? It's got a D in the middle, you know.'

'Yes. I'm always being told things like that,' said Berta, still staring out of the window. 'I had an English governess and she tried to make me speak like you do. I do try, because I've got to go to an English school.

My, my – I wish that island belonged to *me*. I wonder if my pops could buy it.'

George exploded again. '*Buy* it! You donkey, I *told* you it was mine, didn't I?'

Berta turned round in surprise. 'But – you didn't *mean* it, did you?' she said. '*Yours?* But how could it be?'

'It *is* George's,' said Anne. 'It has always belonged to the Kirrin family. That's Kirrin Island. George's father gave it to her, after an adventure we once had.'

Berta stared at George in awe. 'Great snakes! So it *is* yours! Aren't you the lucky one! Will you take me to visit it?'

'I'll see,' said George gruffly, glad to have impressed this American girl so much. Getting her 'Pops' to buy the island indeed! George snorted to herself. What next!

A shout came from the next room. It was Julian. 'Hey, you girls! Are you getting up? We're all too late for a bathe before breakfast this morning. Dick and I have only just woken up.'

'Berta's here!' shouted back Anne. 'We'll get dressed, all of us, and then we'll introduce Berta to you.'

'Are they your brothers?' asked Berta. 'I haven't got any. Or sisters either. I shall be pretty scared of them.'

'You won't be scared of Julian and Dick,' said Anne, proudly. 'You'll wish you had brothers like them. Won't she, George?'

'Yes,' said George, shortly. She was feeling rather annoyed just then because Timmy was standing by Berta, wagging his plumy tail. 'Come here, Timmy. Don't make a nuisance of yourself.'

'Oh, he's not,' said Berta, and patted his big head. 'I like him. He seems simply ENORMOUS after my Sally. But you'll love Sally, George, you really will.

Everyone says how sweet she is – and I've trained her beautifully.'

George took no interest in these remarks at all. She flounced off to wash in the bathroom, but Julian and Dick were there, and there was a lot of yelling and shouting as George tried to make them hurry up and get out. Berta laughed.

'That sounds nice and family-like,' she said. 'You don't get that sort of thing if you're an only child. What do I wear here?'

'Oh – something very simple,' said Anne, looking at the suitcase open on the floor, showing a collection of Berta's clothes. 'That shirt and those jeans will do.'

They were ready just as the gong rang for breakfast. A delicious smell of frying bacon and tomatoes came up the stairs, and Berta sniffed in delight.

'I do like English breakfast,' she said. 'We haven't gotten around to a proper breakfast in America yet! That's bacon and tomatoes I smell, isn't it? My English governess always said that bacon and eggs made the best breakfast in the world, but I guess the one we're going to have will taste pretty good.'

Uncle Quentin was at the table when the children came down. He looked most surprised to see Berta, having quite forgotten that she was coming. 'Who's this?' he said.

'Now Quentin – don't pretend you don't know!' said his wife. 'It's Elbur's girl – your friend Elbur. She came in the middle of the night, but I didn't wake you, you were so sound asleep.'

'Ah yes,' said Uncle Quentin, and he shook hands with the rather scared Berta. 'Glad to have you here, er – let me see now – what's your name?'

'Berta,' said everyone in a chorus.

'Yes, yes – Berta. Sit down, my dear. I know your father well. He's doing some wonderful work.'

Berta beamed. 'He's always at work!' she said. 'He works all through the night sometimes.'

'Does he? Well, what a thing to do!' said Uncle Quentin.

'It's a thing you often do yourself, Quentin,' said his wife, pouring out coffee. 'Though I don't suppose you even realise it.'

Uncle Quentin looked surprised. 'Do I really? Bless us all! Don't I go to bed some nights then?'

Berta laughed. 'You're like my pops! Sometimes he doesn't know what day of the week it is, even! And yet he's supposed to be one of the cleverest guys in the world!'

'Guy?' said Uncle Quentin, surprised, immediately thinking of Firework Night. Everyone laughed. Anne patted her uncle's knee. 'It's all right, Uncle,' she said, 'he's not going to sit on the top of a bonfire!'

But Uncle Quentin was not listening. He had suddenly seen a letter marked 'IMPORTANT' on the top of his pile of correspondence, and he picked it up.

'Well, unless I'm much mistaken, here's a letter from your father,' he said to Berta. 'I'll see what it says.'

He opened the letter and read it to himself. Then he looked up. 'It's all about you – er . . .'

'Her name's Berta,' said Aunt Fanny, patiently.

'About you, Berta,' said Uncle Quentin. 'But I must say your father has some very strange ideas. Yes, very strange.'

'What are they?' asked his wife.

'Well – he says she must be disguised – in case anyone comes to find her here,' said Uncle Quentin. 'And he wants her name changed – and, bless us all, he wants us to buy her boy's clothes – and cut her hair short – and dress her up as a boy!'

Everyone listened in surprise. Berta gave a little squeal.

'I won't! I WON'T be dressed up as a boy! I *won't* have my hair cut off. Don't you dare to make me! I WON'T!'

6 A few upsets

Berta looked so upset that Aunt Fanny acted quickly and firmly. 'Don't bother about that letter now, Quentin,' she said. 'We'll go through it afterwards and decide what to do. Let's have our breakfast in peace.'

'I *won't* have my hair cut off,' said Berta, again. Uncle Quentin was not used to being defied openly like this, and he scowled. He looked at his wife.

'Surely you are not going to let this – er what's her name now – Bertha . . .'

'Berta,' said everyone automatically.

'I said that we would not discuss this till after breakfast,' said Aunt Fanny, in the kind of voice that made everyone, including Uncle Quentin, quite certain that she meant what she said. Her husband folded up the letter and opened the next one, frowning. The children looked at one another.

Berta to be a boy! Goodness! If ever anyone looked less like a boy it was Berta! George was most annoyed. She loved to dress like a boy, but she didn't feel inclined to urge anyone else to! She looked at Berta, who was eating her breakfast with tears in her eyes. What a baby! She wouldn't even *look* like a boy, if she was dressed in boys' clothes. She would just look absolutely silly.

Julian began a conversation with his aunt about the garden. She was grateful to him for breaking up the sudden awkwardness caused by the letter. She was very fond of Julian. 'I can always depend on him,' she thought, and talked gladly of the garden fruit, and who would pick the raspberries for lunch and whether the wasps would eat *all* the plums or not!

Dick joined in, and Anne, and soon Berta did too. Only George and her father remained gloomy. They both looked so exactly alike with solemn, rather frowning expressions that Julian nudged Dick and nodded towards them.

Dick grinned. 'Like father, like daughter!' he said. 'Cheer up, George. Don't you like your breakfast?'

George was just about to answer crossly when Anne gave an exclamation. 'Oh, *look* at Uncle Quentin! He's putting mustard on his toast – Aunt Fanny, stop him – he's just going to eat it!'

Everyone roared with laughter. Aunt Fanny managed to smack her husband's hand down from his mouth, just as he was putting his toast and mustard up to it, reading a letter at the same time.

'Hey – what's the matter?' he said, startled.

'*Quentin* – that's the second time this month you've spread your toast with mustard instead of with marmalade,' said his wife. 'Do have a little sense.'

After that everyone became very cheerful. Uncle Quentin laughed at himself, and George saw the funny side and laughed loudly too, which made Timmy bark, and Berta giggled. Aunt Fanny was quite relieved that her husband had done such a silly thing.

'Do you remember when Father poured custard all over his fried fish once?' George said, entering into the talk for the first time. 'And he said it was the best egg-sauce he had ever tasted?'

The conversation was very animated after that, and Aunt Fanny felt happier. 'You children can clear away and wash up the breakfast things for Joanna,' she said. 'Or two of you can and the others can make the beds with me.'

'What about my little dog?' said Berta, suddenly remembering her again. 'I haven't seen her yet, because I was only just in time for breakfast. Where is she?'

'You can go and get her now,' said Aunt Fanny. 'We've all finished. Are you going to start your work, Quentin?'

'Yes, I am,' said her husband. 'So I don't want any yelling or shouting or barking outside my study door.'

He got up and went out of the room. Berta stood up too. 'Where's the kennel?' she said.

'I'll show you,' said Anne. 'We'll go and get your dog and introduce it to Timmy. Coming, George?'

'You can bring the dog in here, and we'll see what Timmy says,' said George, going all gloomy again. 'If he doesn't like the dog – and he won't – it will have to live out in the kennel.'

'Oh *no*,' said Berta, at once.

'Well, you don't want Timmy to *eat* it, do you?' said George. 'He's very jealous of other dogs in the house. He might go for yours and savage it.'

'Oh *no!*' said Berta, again, looking upset. 'Timmy's nice. He's not a fierce dog.'

'That's all *you* know!' said George. 'Well, I've warned you.'

'Come on,' said Anne, pulling at Berta's sleeve. 'Let's go and fetch Sally. She must be wondering why nobody bothers about her. I bet Timmy won't mind *terribly*.'

As soon as the two had gone out, George spoke in Timmy's ear. 'You don't like strange dogs who want to come and live here, do you, Tim? You'll growl and snarl like anything, won't you? Growl your very fiercest! I know you won't bite but if you could just growl your loudest, that will be enough. Berta will make that Sally-dog live out of doors then!'

Soon she heard footsteps returning, and Anne's voice exclaiming in delight.

'Oh, she's sweet! Oh, what a darling! Sally, you're a pet! Julian, Dick, Aunt Fanny – do come and see Berta's dog!'

Everyone came into the room, led by Berta and Anne. Berta held the dog in her arms.

It was a tiny black poodle, whose woolly fur was cut away here and there to give it a very funny look. Sally was certainly an attractive little thing! Her sharp little nose sniffed all the time she was carried into the room, and her quick little eyes looked everywhere.

Berta put her down, and the little poodle stood there, poised on her dainty feet like a ballet dancer about to perform. Everyone but George exclaimed in delight.

'She's a poppet!'

'Sally! Sally, you're a pet!'

'Oh, a poodle! I do love poodles! They look so knowing.'

Timmy stood by George, sniffing hard to get the smell of this new dog. George had her hand on his collar in case he sprang. His tail was as stiff as a ramrod.

The poodle suddenly saw him. She stared at him out of bright little eyes, quite unafraid. Then she pulled away from Berta's hand and trotted right over to Timmy, her funny little tail wagging merrily.

Timmy backed a little in surprise. The poodle danced all round him on her toes, and gave a little whimpering bark, which said as plainly as possible, I want to play with you!

Timmy sprang. He leapt in the air and came down with a thud on his big paws, and the little poodle dodged. Timmy's tail began to wag wildly. He sprang again in play, and almost knocked the little poodle over. He barked as if to say 'Sorry, I didn't mean that!'

Then he and the poodle played a most ridiculous game of dodge and run, and although one or two chairs went flying nobody minded – they were all laughing so much at the sight of the quick little poodle leading Timmy such a dance.

At last Sally was tired and sat down in a corner. Timmy pranced about in front of her, showing off. Then he went up to her and sniffed her nose. He licked it gently, and then lay down in front of her, gazing at her adoringly.

Anne gave a little squeal of laughter. 'He's gazing at Sally exactly as he gazes at you, George!' she cried.

But George was not at all pleased. In fact she was quite astounded. To think that Timmy should *welcome* another dog! To think that he should behave like this when she had told him to do the opposite!

'Aren't they sweet together?' said Berta, pleased. 'I *thought* Timmy would like Sally. Of course Sally is a pedigree dog, and cost a lot of money – and Timmy's only a mongrel. I expect he thinks she's *wunnerful*.'

'Oh, Tim may be a mongrel, but he's absolutely wunnerful too,' said Dick, hastily, pronouncing the word like Berta, to try and get a laugh. He saw George's scowl, and knew how cross she felt at hearing her beloved Timmy compared with a pedigree dog. 'He's a magnificent fellow, aren't you, Timmy?' went on Dick. 'Sally may be a darling, but you're worth more than a *hundred* darlings, aren't you?'

'I think he's beautiful,' said Berta, looking down at Timmy. 'He's got the loveliest eyes I ever did see.'

George began to feel a little better. She called Timmy. 'You're making rather a fool of yourself,' she said to him.

'Now that Timmy and Sally are going to be friends, can I have Sally to sleep on my bed at night, like

George has Timmy?' said Berta. 'Please say yes, Aunt Fanny.'

'No,' said George at once. 'Mother, I won't have that. I won't!'

'Well, we'll see what we can do about it,' said her mother. 'Sally was quite happy in the kennel last night, I must say.'

'I'm going to have her sleep with me,' said Berta, scowling at George. 'My father will pay you a lot of money to make me happy. He told me he would.'

'Don't be silly, Berta,' said Aunt Fanny, firmly. 'This isn't a question of money. Now, leave this for a little while, please, and go and do your jobs, all of you. And then we must consider your father's letter, Berta, and see exactly what he wants done. We must certainly try to follow his advice about you.'

'But I don't want to . . .' began Berta, and then felt a firm hand on her arm. It was Julian.

'Come on, kid,' he said. 'Be your age! Remember you're a guest here and put on a few of your best manners. We like American children – but not *spoilt* ones!'

Berta had quite a shock to hear Julian speaking like this. She looked up at him and he grinned down at her. She felt near tears, but she smiled back.

'You haven't any brothers to keep you in your place,' said Julian, linking his arm in hers. 'Well, from now on, while you're here, Dick and I are your brothers, and you've got to toe the line, just like Anne. See? What about it?'

Berta felt that there was nothing in the world she would like better than having Julian for a brother! He was big and tall and had twinkling kindly eyes that made Berta feel he was as responsible and trustable as her father.

Aunt Fanny smiled to herself. Julian always knew

the best thing to say and do. Now he would take Berta
in hand and see that she didn't upset the household too
much. She was glad. It wasn't easy to run a big family
like this, with a scientist husband to cope with, unless
everyone pulled together!

'You go and help Aunt Fanny with the beds,' said
Julian to Berta. 'And take your Sally-dog with you.
She's great! But so is Timmy, and don't you forget it!'

7 *A little conference*

Peace reigned in the house for a little while. George and Anne went to help the cook with the washing-up. Joanna was pleased, because with eight people in the house, including herself, there was a lot to do.

She had been very astonished that morning to find a fifth child added to the household, but had been told that after breakfast she could go into the sitting-room and hear an explanation! Joanna must certainly be in the secret too!

Upstairs Berta was helping with the beds – not very successfully because she was not used to doing things for herself. But she was very willing to learn and Aunt Fanny was quite pleased with her. Timmy and Sally darted about together and made things rather more difficult than they need have been, popping under beds and out again at top speed.

'I'm glad Timmy likes Sally,' said Berta. 'I knew he would. I can't think why George thought he wouldn't. George is funny, I think.'

'Not really,' said Aunt Fanny. 'She hasn't any brothers or sisters to rub off her corners, and she didn't even know her three cousins till a few years ago, or go to school. Lonely people aren't so easy to get on with as others – but she is great fun now, as you will soon find out.'

'I'm an only child too,' said Berta. 'But I've always had plenty of other children to play with. My pop saw to that. He's wunnerful – I mean wonDERful. I'll say that word "wonDERful" twenny times, then maybe, I'll get it right.'

'Well, say the word "twenty" as well!' said Aunt Fanny. 'It has a letter T at the end as well as at the beginning, you know. It's "twenTY" not "twenny". But don't make yourself *too* English. It's nice to have a change!'

'WonDERful, wonDERful, wonDERful! TwenTY, twenTY!' chanted Berta, as she made the beds. Dick looked into the room and chuckled.

'Great snakes!' he said, with a grin, and an American accent. 'You shore are wunnerful, baby!'

'Don't be so silly, Dick,' said his aunt, laughing. 'Now – I think we've finished all we have to do, Berta. We'll go downstairs and have a conference. Tell the others, will you?'

Berta, followed closely by Sally, who was also followed closely by an adoring Timmy, went to tell Dick and Julian, and then George and Anne. George was not too pleased with Timmy.

'Where have you been?' she said. 'Can't you stop running about after Sally? She'll get very very tired of you!'

'Wuff!' said Sally, in a high little bark, not at all like Timmy's deep 'Woof!'

Soon all five children and the two dogs, and also Joanna, were in the sitting-room with Aunt Fanny. Berta began to look a little nervous.

Aunt Fanny had the letter that Berta's father had sent. She did not read it out to the children, but told them what was in it. She also explained to Joanna about Berta.

'Joanna, you have always known what important work my husband does,' she said. 'Well, Berta's father does the same kind of work in America, and he and Quentin are working on a great new scheme together.'

'Oh yes,' said Joanna, very much interested.

'Berta's father has been warned by the police that it is possible Berta may be kidnapped and held to ransom, not for money, but for the scientific secrets that he knows,' went on Aunt Fanny. 'So she has been sent to us to be kept safe for three weeks. By that time the scheme will be finished and made public. Berta is going to the same school as Anne and George, and it is a good idea to let them know one another first.'

Joanna nodded. 'I understand that,' she said. 'I think we can keep Berta safe, don't you?'

'Yes,' said Aunt Fanny. 'But her father has now put up some further ideas that he wants us to follow. He says it would be best to disguise her as a boy . . .'

'Jolly good idea,' interrupted Dick.

'And to give her another name – a boy's name,' said Aunt Fanny. 'He wants her to have her hair cut short and . . .'

'Oh please not that!' begged Berta, shaking back her fair, wavy hair. 'I'd hate it. Girls with short hair like boys look so silly, they . . .'

Anne nudged her and frowned. Berta stopped hurriedly, remembering that George had curly hair cut as short as any boy.

'I think we'll have to do what your father says,' said Aunt Fanny. 'This is very important, Berta. You see, if anyone *should* come here looking for you, thinking of kidnapping, they would never recognise you if you were looking exactly like a boy.'

'But my hair,' said Berta, almost in tears. 'How *could* Pops says I'm to have my hair off? He always said it was wunnerful!'

Nobody liked to point out that there was a D in wonderful just then! Berta was really so very upset about her hair.

'Your hair will grow quickly enough,' said Aunt Fanny.

'Her *head's* a good shape,' said Julian, looking at it consideringly. 'She should look nice with short hair.'

Berta cheered up. If Julian thought that, then it wouldn't be so bad.

'But what about clothes?' she said, remembering this point with a look of horror. 'Girls look frightful in boys' clothes. Pops always said so till now.'

'You won't look any worse than George does,' said Dick. 'She's got on a boy's jersey, boy's jeans and boy's shoes this very minute!'

'I think she looks awful,' said Berta, obstinately, and George scowled.

'Well, I think *you*'d look horrible,' she said. 'You wouldn't even *look* like a boy, you'd look little-girlish, silly little sissy-boy. *I* think it's a stupid idea to put you into boy's clothes!'

'Aha! Our George wants to be the only one!' said Dick, slyly, and quickly got out of the way of a punch from the furious George.

'Well,' said Julian. 'I'll go out and buy some things for Berta this morning, so that's settled. What about her hair? Shall *I* cut it short?'

Aunt Fanny was amused at Julian's high-handed way of dealing with Berta and her troubles, and even more amused to see that Berta did not even argue with Julian.

'You can certainly go shopping for Berta if you like,' she said. 'But I'd rather you didn't cut her hair. You'd make her look a scarerow!'

'I don't mind if Julian cuts it,' said Berta, surprisingly meek all at once.

'I shall cut it for you myself,' said Aunt Fanny. 'Now – what about a boy's name? We can't call you Berta any more, that's certain.'

'I'd rather not have a boy's name,' said Berta. 'It's silly for a girl to be called by a boy's name, like George.'

'If you *mean* to be rude to me, I'll . . .' began George, but got no farther. Julian and Dick had burst into laughter.

'Oh George – you and Berta will be the death of us!' said Julian. 'Here are you doing all you can to *pretend* to be a boy – and here is Berta doing all she can to get *out* of it! For goodness sake, let's settle the matter without any more bickering. We'll call Berta Robert.'

'No – that's too like Berta,' said Dick. 'It ought to be a completely different name. We'll call her a good plain boy's name like Jim or Tom or John.'

'No,' said Berta. 'I don't like any of them. Let me have my second name, please.'

'What's that? Another girl's name?' asked Julian.

'Yes. But it's used for a boy too, only then it's spelt differently,' said Berta. 'It's Lesley. It's a nice name, I think.'

'Lesley. Yes – it rather suits you,' said Julian. 'It suits you better than Berta. We'll call you Lesley – and people will think it's Leslie spelt l-i-e at the end, and not l-e-y. All right. Everything's settled.'

'Not quite,' said his aunt. 'I just want to say that you mustn't let Berta – I mean Lesley – out of your sight at all. And you must report at once any mysterious happening or any stranger you see. The local police here know that we have Lesley with us, and why – and anything can be reported to them at once. They also are keeping a good look-out, of course.'

'This almost sounds as if we're in the middle of an adventure!' said Dick, looking pleased.

'I hope not,' said his aunt. 'I don't imagine that anyone will ever guess Berta – I mean Lesley – is anything more than she will appear to be – a boy friend of yours and Julian's, come to stay for a while. Dear me, it's going to be difficult to refer to her as him all the time!'

'It certainly is,' said Julian, standing up. 'If you'll give me some money, Aunt Fanny, I'll go and do a little shopping for Lesley. What size do you think HE needs?'

Everyone laughed. 'HE wears size three shoes,' said Joanna smiling. 'I noticed that this morning.'

'And HE will have to get used to doing his coat buttons up on the right-hand side instead of on the left,' said Anne, joining in the fun.

'SHE will soon get used to that,' said George. 'Won't SHE, Timmy?'

'Don't spoil it all now, George,' said Julian. 'A slip of the tongue, saying SHE instead of HE, might lead to danger for Ber – I mean Lesley.'

'Yes, I know,' said George. 'It's just that she'll never look like a boy, and . . .'

'I don't *want* to look like a boy,' said Berta. 'I think *you* look . . .'

'Here we go again!' said Julian. 'Stop it, Lesley, stop it, George. George, you'd better come out and help me to get the things for Lesley. Come on. And take that scowl off your face. You look like a sulky girl!'

That made George alter her face at once. She couldn't help grinning at the artful Julian.

'I'm coming,' she said. 'Goodbye, Berta. When we come back, you'll be Leslie, haircut and all!'

She and Julian went off. Anne fetched her aunt's sharpest scissors and draped a big towel round Berta's shoulders. Berta looked as if she was going to cry.

'Cheer up,' said Dick. 'You're going to look angelic with short hair! Begin, Aunt Fanny. Let's see what she's like with shorn locks.'

'Sit quite still,' said Aunt Fanny and began. Clip-

clip-clip! The wavy golden hair fell to the floor in big strands and Berta began to weep in earnest. 'My hair! I can't bear this. Oh, my hair!'

Soon most of it was on the floor, and Aunt Fanny began to clip what was left as best she could, to make it look as boyish as possible. She made a very good job of it indeed. Dick and Anne watched with the greatest interest.

'There! It's done!' said Aunt Fanny at last. 'Stop crying, Lesley – and let's have a look at you!'

8   *A transformation*

Berta stood in the middle of the floor, blinking her tears away. Anne gave a gasp.

'You know – it's *very* odd – but she does look rather like a boy – a very, very good-looking boy!'

'An angelic boy,' said Dick. 'A choirboy or something. She looks smashing! Who would have thought it?'

Aunt Fanny was very struck with Berta's appearance too. 'It's certainly very odd,' she said. 'But there's no doubt about it – when she's – I mean he's – dressed in boy's clothes, he'll make a fine boy. Better than George, actually, because her hair's *really* too curly for a boy.'

Berta went to the looking-glass on the wall. She gave a wail. 'I look awful! I don't know myself! Nobody would EVER recognise me!'

'Splendid!' said Dick, at once. 'You've hit the nail right on the head. Nobody *would* recognise you now. Your father was quite right to say, cut your hair off and dress up as a boy. Any prowling kidnapper would never think *you* were Berta, the pretty little girl.'

'I'd rather be kidnapped than look like this,' wept Berta. 'What will the girls at your school say, Anne, when they see me?'

'They don't say anything to George about her short hair, and they won't say anything to you,' said Anne.

'Stop crying, Bert – er – Lesley,' said Aunt Fanny. 'You make me feel quite miserable. You've been very good to sit so still all that time. Now I really must think of a little reward for you.'

Berta stopped crying at once. 'Please,' she said, 'there's only one thing I want now. I want Sally-dog to sleep with me.'

'Oh dear, Ber – er Lesley – I really *can't* have another dog in that little bedroom,' said poor Aunt Fanny. 'And George would make things most unpleasant if I did.'

'Aunt Fanny – Sally is a very very good guard for me,' said Berta. 'She barks at the very slightest sound. I'd feel safe with her in the bedroom.'

'I'd like you to have her,' said Aunt Fanny, 'but . . .'

Joanna had come into the room to put away some things and had heard the conversation. She stared in admiration at Berta's neat golden head, and then made a suggestion.

'Berta could have her camp-bed in *my* room,' she said. 'I don't mind the dog a bit, she can have her and welcome, she's a pet, that little poodle. It's very crowded in the girls' room now, with three beds in it, and my room's a nice big one. So, if Berta doesn't mind sharing it, she's welcome.'

'Oh Joanna – that's good of you,' said Aunt Fanny, relieved at such a simple solution. 'Also, your room is up in the attic – it would be *very* difficult for kidnappers to find their way there – and nobody would think of looking into your room for one of the children.'

'*Thank* you, Joanna, you're just *wunnerful*!' said Berta in delight. 'Sally, do you hear that? You'll be sleeping on my feet tonight, like Timmy does on George's.'

'I don't really approve of that, you know, Berta,' said Aunt Fanny. 'Oh dear – I called you Berta again. Lesley, I mean. What a muddle I'm going to get into!

Anne, get the dustpan and sweep up the hair on the floor.'

When Julian and George came back there was no sign of the golden hair on the floor. They put their parcels down on the table and shouted for Aunt Fanny. 'Mother!' called George. 'Aunt Fanny!' shouted Julian.

She came running downstairs with Berta and Anne and Dick. Julian and George looked at Berta, thunderstruck. 'Gosh – is it *really* you, Berta?' said Julian. 'I simply didn't recognise you!'

'Why – you *do* look like a boy!' said George. 'I never thought you would.'

'A jolly good-looking boy,' said Julian. 'Well, your father was right. It's the best disguise you could have!'

'Where are the clothes?' asked Berta, rather pleased at all the interest in her looks. They opened the parcels and pulled out the things.

They were not really very exciting – a boy's anorak in navy blue, two pairs of boy's jeans, two grey jerseys, a few shirts, a tie and a pullover without sleeves.

'And shoes and socks,' said George. 'But we decided you'd got plenty of socks that would do, so we only bought one pair of those. Oh – and here's a boy's cap! We bought it just for fun.'

Berta put on the cap at once. There were squeals of laughter from everyone. 'It suits her! She's got it on at just the right angle. She looks a real boy!'

'*You* put it on, George,' said Berta, and George took it, eager to share in the admiration. But it looked ridiculous on her curls, and wouldn't sit down flat as it should. Everyone hooted.

'It makes you look a girl! Take it off!'

George took it off in disappointment. How very aggravating that this girl Berta should make a better boy than she did! She threw the cap on the table, half-cross that they had bought it.

'Go upstairs and put some of the things on,' said Aunt Fanny, amused at all these goings-on. Up went Berta obediently, and soon came down again, neatly arrayed in jeans, grey shirt and blue tie.

Everyone roared with laughter. Berta was now quite enjoying herself and paraded round the room, her cap tilted on one side of her head.

'She looks like a very tidy, neat little boy, a good and most angelic child!' said Julian. 'Dear Lesley, you must get yourself just a little dirty – you look too good to be true.'

'I don't like getting dirty,' said Berta. 'I think . . .'

But what she thought nobody knew because at that moment the door opened and Uncle Quentin came into the room.

'I'd like to know how you think I can do my work with all this hooting and cackling going on,' he began, and then he suddenly saw Berta, and stopped.

'Who's this?' he said, looking Berta up and down.

'Don't you know, Father?' said George.

'Of course not. Never seen him in my life before!' said her father. 'Don't tell me it's somebody else come to stay.'

'It's Berta,' said Anne, with a giggle.

'Berta – now who's Berta?' said Uncle Quentin, frowning. 'I seem to have heard that name before.'

'The girl you thought might be kidnapped,' explained Dick.

'Oh *Berta* – Elbur's girl!' said Uncle Quentin. 'I remember *her* all right. But who's *this*? This boy? I've never seen *him* before. What's your name, boy?'

'Lesley,' said Berta. 'But I was Berta when you saw me at breakfast.'

'Good heavens!' said Uncle Quentin, amazed. 'What a – what a transformation! Why, your own father wouldn't know you. I hope I remember who you are. Keep reminding me, if I don't.'

Off he went, back to his study. The children laughed, and Aunt Fanny had to laugh too.

'By the way,' she said, 'I want you all to have lunch at home today, because it's really too late now to start making sandwiches for a picnic; it's only cold ham and salad, so don't get *too* hungry, will you?'

'Is there time for a bathe?' asked Julian, looking at his watch.

'Yes – if you'll come in about twelve o'clock and pick the fruit for a pudding for lunch,' said his aunt. 'It takes ages to pick enough for eight people, and Joanna and I have a lot to do today.'

'Right. We'll go for a bathe now, and then we'll ALL pick fruit,' said Julian. 'Bags I pick the plums. The raspberries are such fiddly little things.'

'Have you a swimsuit, Berta, I mean Lesley?' asked George.

'Yes. It's an absolutely plain one, so I'll be all right in it,' said Berta. 'Hurray, I shan't need to wear a cap. Boys never do.'

Berta's cases were now all in Joanna's big room and she ran to get into her swimsuit.

'Bring your anorak and a towel,' yelled George, and went into her own room with Anne.

'I bet Berta can't swim,' she said. 'That will be a pity. We'll have to teach her.'

'Well, don't duck her too often!' said Anne, seeing a look in George's eye that was not too kindly. 'Blow – my swimsuit isn't here – I'm sure I brought it in from the clothes-line.'

It took quite a while to find it, and the boys and Berta had already gone down to the beach with Sally by the time Anne and George were ready to follow with the impatient Timmy.

They were down on the beach at last, and there was Sally-dog guarding the anoraks belonging to Julian, Dick and Berta. She was lying on them, and she even dared to growl at Timmy when he came near.

George laughed. 'Growl back, Timmy! Don't let a little snippet like that cheek you. Growl back!'

But Timmy wouldn't. He just sat down out of reach of Sally, and looked at her sadly. Wasn't she friends with him any more?

'Where are the others?' said Anne, shading her eyes from the glare of the sun and looking out to sea. 'Goodness, how far out they've swum! That *can't* be Berta with them, surely!'

George looked out over the stretch of blue sea at once. She saw three heads bobbing. Yes, Berta *was* out there!

'She must be a jolly good swimmer,' said Anne, admiringly. 'I couldn't swim out as far as that. We were wrong about Berta. She swims like a fish!'

George said nothing. She ran to the waves, plunged through a big one just as it was curling over, and swam out strongly. She couldn't *believe* that it was Berta out there! And if it was, the boys must be helping her!

But it *was* Berta. Her golden head glistened wet in the water, and she shouted in glee as she swam.

'This is great! This is wunnerful! Gee, I'm enjoying this! Hi there, George – isn't the water warm?'

Julian and Dick grinned at the panting George. 'Lesley's a fine swimmer,' said Dick. 'Gosh, I thought she was going to race me at one time. She'd beat *you*, George!'

'She wouldn't,' said George, but all the same she didn't challenge Berta to race!

It was fun to be five, fun to chase one another in the

sea, to swim under the water and grab somebody's leg. And Anne laughed till she choked when she saw somebody heave themselves out of the water right on to George's back, and duck her well and truly.

It was Berta! And what was more, the angry George couldn't catch her afterwards. Berta could swim much too fast!

9 A sudden telephone call

Berta soon settled down happily with the Five. George couldn't bear to think that the girl had to be dressed like a boy, but her jealousy wore off a little as the days went by – though she couldn't help feeling annoyed that Berta proved to be such a good swimmer!

She could dive well too, and swim under water even longer than the boys could, much to their surprise.

'Oh well, you see, back home, we've got a pool in our garden,' she said. 'A wonDERful pool, gee, you should see it. And I learnt to swim in it when I was two. Pops always called me a water-baby.'

Berta ate just as much as the others, although she was not so sturdy and well built. She was loud in her praise of the meals, and this pleased Aunt Fanny and Joanna very much.

'You're getting fatter, Lesley,' said Aunt Fanny a week later, looking at her as she sat eating her lunch with the others. 'And what is better still – you're getting a really good sun-tan. You're almost as brown as the others!'

'Yes. I thought so too,' said Berta, pleased.

'It's a good thing you caught the sun so easily,' said Aunt Fanny. 'Now, if any kidnappers come round looking for a long-haired pale-faced American girl, they would take one look at the lot of you and off they would go! Nobody would guess you were Berta!'

'All the same, I'd much rather *be* Berta,' said Berta. 'I still don't like pretending to be a boy. It's silly, and it makes me *feel* silly. Anyway, thank goodness my hair's growing a bit longer. I don't look *quite* so much like a boy now!'

'Dear me, you're right,' said Aunt Fanny, and everyone looked at Berta. 'I shall have to cut it short again.'

'Gosh!' said Berta. 'Why did I say that? You wouldn't have noticed if I hadn't mentioned it. Let it grow again, please, Aunt Fanny. I've been here a week and there isn't even a *smell* of a kidnapper – and I reckon there won't be either!'

But Aunt Fanny was firm about the hair, and after the meal she made Berta sit still while she clipped it a little shorter. It was not a bit curly like George's, and now that it was short, the wave had almost gone from it. She really did look like a good clean little boy!

'Rather a wishy-washy one!' said George, unkindly, but everyone knew what she meant.

Sally the poodle was a great success. Even George couldn't go on disliking the happy, dancing little dog. She trotted and capered about on her slim little legs, and Timmy was her adoring slave.

'She always looks as if she's running about on tip-toe,' said Anne, and so she did. She made friends with everyone, even the paper-boy, who was really scared of dogs.

Uncle Quentin was the only one who didn't get used to Berta and Sally. When he met them together, Berta so like a small boy, Sally at her heels, he stopped and stared.

'Now let me see – who are you?' he said. 'Yes – you're Berta!'

'No – he's LESLEY!' everyone would say.

'You must *not* call her Berta, dear,' said his wife. 'You really must not. It's a funny thing that you never could remember she was Berta, and now that we've made her into Lesley, you immediately remember she's Berta!'

'Well, I must say you've made her look exactly like a boy,' said Uncle Quentin, much to George's annoyance. George was beginning to be afraid that Berta looked more boyish than she did! 'Well, I hope you're having a good time with the others, er – er . . .'

'*Lesley* is the name,' said Aunt Fanny with a little laugh. 'Quentin, do try and remember.'

Another day passed peacefully by, and the five children and two dogs were out of doors all day long, swimming, boating, exploring, really enjoying themselves.

Berta wanted to go over to Kirrin Island, but George kept making excuses not to go. 'Don't be mean,' said Dick. 'We *all* want to go. It's ages since we went. It's just that you don't want to let Lesley do something she'd like to do!'

'It isn't,' said George. 'Perhaps we'll go tomorrow.'

But when tomorrow came something happened that upset their plans for going to Kirrin Island. A telephone call came for Uncle Quentin, and immediately he was in a panic.

'Fanny! Fanny, where are you?' he called. 'Pack my bag at once. At once, do you hear?'

His wife came running down the stairs at top speed. 'Quentin, why? What's happened?'

'Elbur's found a mistake in our calculations,' said Uncle Quentin. 'What nonsense! There's no mistake. None at all.'

'But why can't he come *here* and work it out with you?' asked his wife. 'Why have *you* got to rush off like this? Tell him to come here, Quentin. I'll find him a bed somehow.'

'He says he doesn't want to, while his daughter – his daughter – what's her name now?'

'*Lesley*,' said his wife. 'All right, don't bother to explain. I see now that it would be foolish for him to come while Lesley's here – she'd be calling him Pops, and . . .'

'Pops?' said her husband, startled. 'What do you mean – Pops?'

'It's what she calls her father, dear,' said Aunt Fanny, patiently. 'Anyway, he's quite right. It would be foolish to hide Lesley here so well, and then have everyone hear her calling him Pops, and him calling her Berta – if any kidnappers followed him, they would soon find out where his daughter was – here, with our four!'

'Yes – that's what I was trying to tell you,' said her husband, impatiently. 'Anyway I must go to Elbur straight away. So pack my bag, please. I'll be back in two days' time.

'In that case I'll go with you, Quentin,' said his wife. 'I could do with a quiet two days – and you're not much good when you're alone, are you – losing your socks, and forgetting to have your shoes cleaned, and . . .'

Her husband gave a sudden smile that lit up his face and made him seem quite young. 'Will you really come with me? I thought you'd hate to leave the children.'

'It's only for two days,' said his wife. 'And Joanna is very good with them. I'll arrange that they shall go out on all-day picnics in the boat – they'll be quite safe then. If any kidnappers *were* around they'd find it difficult to snatch Lesley out of a boat! But I'm beginning not to believe that tale of Elbur's. He just got into a panic when he heard the rumour, I expect.'

The children were told of the sudden decision when they got back to lunch that day. Joanna had to tell them, because Aunt Fanny and her husband had already departed, complete with two suitcases, one containing precious papers and the other clothes for two days.

'Gosh!' said Julian, surprised. 'I hope nothing horrid's happened.'

'Oh no – it was just a sudden telephone call from Lesley's father,' said Joanna, smiling at Berta. 'He had to see your uncle in a hurry – about some figures.'

'Why didn't Pops come down here – then he could have seen *me*?' demanded Berta at once.

'Because everyone would have known who you are, then,' said Dick. 'We're *hiding* you, don't forget!'

'Oh yes – well I do believe I *had* forgotten,' said Berta, rather surprised at herself. 'It's so *lovely* down here in Kirrin with you all. The days seem to *swim* by!'

'Your mother said you had better go off on all-day picnics in the boat,' said Joanna to George. 'That was to make things easy for me, of course. But I don't mind what you do – you can come back to lunch each day, if you like.'

'I do so like you, Joanna!' said Berta, giving the surprised cook a sudden hug. 'You're a real honey!'

'In fact, she's quite wunnerful!' said Dick. 'It's all right, Joanna – we'll go out for the midday meal, *and* for tea, till my aunt comes back. And we'll make the sandwiches and pack up everything ourselves.'

'Well, that's nice of you,' said Joanna. 'Why don't you go across to Kirrin Island for the day? Lesley keeps wanting to go.'

Berta grinned at Joanna.

'We'll go if the boat is ready,' said George, rather reluctantly. 'You know James is mending one of the rowlocks. We'll go and see if it's finished.'

They all went to see, but James was not there. His father was working on another boat, over by the jetty, and he called to them.

'Do you want my James? He's gone off in his uncle's boat for a day's fishing. He said to tell you the rowlock's not mended yet, but he'll do it for certain tonight when he comes back.'

'Right. Thank you,' called back Julian. Berta looked very disappointed. 'Cheer up,' he said. 'We'll be able to go tomorrow.'

'We shan't,' said Berta, mournfully. 'Something else will happen to prevent us – or Geroge will think of another excuse not to go. Gee, if I had a wunnerful – wonDERful – island like that, I'd go and *live* on it.'

They went back to Kirrin Cottage and packed up a very good lunch for themselves. Berta's father had sent down a parcel of American goodies three days before, and they meant to try them.

'Snick-snacks!' said Dick, reading the name on a tin. 'Shrimp, lobster, crab and a dozen other things all in one tin. Sounds good. We'll make sandwiches with this!'

'Gorgies,' said Anne, reading the name on another tin. 'What a peculiar name! Oh – I suppose it's something you *gorge* yourself with. Let's open it.'

They opened half a dozen tins with most exciting names and made themselves so many sandwiches that Joanna exclaimed in amazement. 'How ever many have you made for each of you?'

'Twenny each – I mean twenTY,' said Berta. 'But we won't be back to lunch *or* tea, Joanna. I guess we'll be plenny hungry.'

'PlenTy!' chorused everyone, and Berta obediently repeated the word, a grin on her sun-tanned face.

What a day they had! They walked for miles and picnicked in a shady wood near a little stream that bubbled along nearby, sounding very cool and enticing. They decided to sit with their feet in it as they ate, and Anne gave continual little squeals because she said the water tickled the soles of her feet.

They were so tired when they got home that night that it was all they could do to eat their supper and stagger upstairs to bed.

'I shan't wake till half past twelve tomorrow morning,' yawned Dick. 'Oh my poor feet! Gosh, I'm so tired I shall probably fall asleep cleaning my teeth.'

'What a peaceful night!' said Anne, looking out of her window. 'Well – sleep tight, everyone. I don't expect any of us will open an eye till late tomorrow morning. I know I shan't!'

But she did. She opened both eyes very wide indeed in the middle of the night.

10 A puzzling thing

All was quiet at Kirrin Cottage. The two boys slept soundly in their room, and George and Anne slept without stirring in theirs. Berta was up in Joanna's attic room, and hadn't moved since she had flopped into bed.

Timmy was on George's feet, as usual, and Sally the poodle was curled up in the crook of Berta's knees, looking like a ball of black wool! Nobody stirred.

A black cloud crept up the sky and blotted out the stars one by one. Then a low roll of thunder came. It was far off, and only a rumble, but it woke both the dogs, and it woke Anne too.

She opened her eyes, wondering what the noise was. Then she knew – it was thunder.

'Oh, I hope a storm won't come and break up this wonderful weather!' she thought, as she lay and listened. She turned towards the open window and looked for the stars, but there were none to see.

'Well, if a storm's coming, I'll go and watch it at the window,' thought Anne. 'It should be a magnificent sight over Kirrin Bay. I'm so hot too – I'd like a breath of fresh air at the window!'

She got quietly out of bed and padded over to the open window. She leaned out, sniffing the cool air outside. The night was very dark indeed, because of the great black cloud.

The thunder came again, but not very near – just a low growl. Timmy jumped off George's bed and went to join Anne. He put his great paws up on the window-sill and looked out solemnly over the bay.

And then both he and Anne heard another sound – a faraway chug-chug-chug-chug-chug.

'It's a motorboat,' said Anne, listening. 'Isn't it Timmy? Someone's having a very late trip! Can you see any ship-lights, Tim? I can't.'

The engine of the motorboat cut out just then, and there was complete silence except for the swish-swash-swish of the waves on the beach. Anne strained her eyes to see if she could spot any light anywhere to show where the motorboat was. It sounded quite far out in the bay. Why had it stopped on the water? Why hadn't it gone to the jetty?

Then she did see a light, but a very faint one, right out at the entrance of the bay, about the middle. It shone for a while, moved here and there, and then disappeared. Anne was puzzled.

'Surely that's just about where Kirrin Island is?' she whispered to Timmy. 'Is anyone there? Has the motorboat gone there, do you suppose? Well, we'll listen to see if it leaves again and goes away.'

But no further sound came from across the bay, and no light shone either. 'Perhaps the motorboat is *behind* Kirrin Island,' thought Anne, suddenly. 'And then I wouldn't be able to see any lights on it – the island would hide the boat *and* its lights. But what was that *moving* light I saw? *Was* it someone on the island? Oh dear, my eyes are getting so sleepy again that I can hardly keep them open. Perhaps I didn't hear or see anything after all!'

There was no more thunder, and no lightning at all. The big black cloud began to thin out and one or two stars appeared in the gaps. Anne yawned and crawled into bed. Timmy jumped back on George's bed and curled himself up with a little sigh.

In the morning Anne had almost forgotten her watch at the open window the night before. It was only when Joanna mentioned that a big storm had burst over a town fifty miles away that Anne remembered the thunder she had heard.

'Oh!' she said, suddenly. 'Yes – *I* heard thunder too, and I got out of bed, hoping to watch a storm. But it didn't come. And I heard a motorboat far out in the bay, but I couldn't see any lights – except for a faint, moving one I thought was on Kirrin Island.'

George sat up in her chair as if she had had an electric shock. 'On Kirrin Island! Whatever do you mean? Nobody's there. *Nobody's* allowed there!'

'Well – I may have been mistaken,' said Anne. 'I was so very sleepy. I didn't hear the motorboat go away. I just went back to bed.'

'You *might* have woken me, if you thought you saw a light on my island,' said George. 'You really might!'

'Oh, Anne – it wouldn't be kidnappers, would it!' said Joanna, at once.

Julian laughed. 'No, Joanna. What would be the use of them going to Kirrin Island? They couldn't do any kidnapping there, in full view of all the houses round the bay!'

'I guess it was only a dream, Anne,' said Berta. 'I guess you heard the thunder in your sleep, and it turned into the sound of a motorboat chugging – dreams *do* that sort of thing. I know once I left the tap running in my basin when I went to sleep, and I dreamed all night long I was riding over the Niagara Falls!'

Everyone laughed. Berta could be very droll at times. 'If the boat's ready, we'll certainly go over to Kirrin Island today,' said George. 'If any trippers are there I'll send Timmy after them!'

'There will only be the rabbits,' said Dick. 'I wonder

if there are still hundreds there – my word, last time we went they were so tame that we nearly fell over them!'

'Yes – but we didn't have Timmy with us,' said Anne. 'George, it *will* be nice to go to Kirrin Island again. We'll have to tell Lesley about the adventures we've had there.'

They washed up after breakfast, made the beds and did their rooms. Joanna put her head round Julian's bedroom door.

'Will you want a packed lunch for a picnic again, Julian?' she said. 'If you don't, I can get you a nice bit of cold ham for lunch. The grocer's just rung up.'

'If the boat's mended, we're going over to the island, Joanna,' said Julian. 'And then we'd like a packed lunch. But if we don't go, we'll stay for lunch. It will be easier for you in a way, won't it? We all got up so late this morning that there's not much time to make sandwiches and pick fruit and so on.'

'Well, you tell me, as soon as you know about the boat,' said Joanna, and disappeared.

George came in. 'I'm going to see if the boat is mended,' she said. 'I'll only be gone a minute. Joanna wants to know.'

She was back almost at once. 'It's not ready,' she said, disappointed. 'But it will be ready at two o'clock this afternoon. So we'll have lunch here, shall we, and then go over to the island afterwards? We'll pack up a picnic tea.'

'Right,' said Julian. 'I vote we bathe from the beach this morning, then. The tide will be nice and high and we can have some fun with the big breakers.'

'And also keep an eye on James to see that he keeps his word about the boat,' said Dick.

So, when all their jobs were finished – and they were very conscientious about them – the five children and the two dogs went off down to the beach. It was a little cooler after the thunder, but not much, and they were quite warm enough in their swimsuits, with an anorak to wear after a bathe.

'There's nothing nicer than to feel hot and go into the sea and get cool, and then come out and get hot in the sun again, and then go back into the sea,' began Berta.

'You say that every single day!' said George. 'It's like a record! Still, I must say that I agree with you! Come on – let's have a jolly good swim!'

They all plunged through the big, curling breakers, squealing as the water dashed over this bodies, cold and stinging. They chased one another, swam under water and grabbed at the legs swimming there, floated on their backs, and wished they hadn't forgotten to bring the big red rubber ball with them. But nobody wanted to go and fetch it so they had to do without it.

Timmy and Sally raced about in the shallow waves at the edge of the sea. Timmy was a fine swimmer, but Sally didn't much like the water, so they always played together at the edge. They really were most amusing to watch.

The dogs were glad when the children came panting out of the water. They lay down on the warm beach and Timmy flopped down beside George. She pushed him away.

'You smell of seaweed,' she said. 'Pooh!'

After a while Dick sat up to pull on his anorak. He gazed over the bay to where Kirrin Island lay basking in the sun and gave a sudden exclamation.

'I say! Look, all of you!'

Everyone sat up. 'There's someone on Kirrin Island, though I can't see them,' said Dick. 'Someone lying down, looking through binoculars at our beach. Can you see the sun glittering on the glasses?'

'Yes!' said Julian. 'You're right! Someone must be

using binoculars to examine this beach. We can't see them as you say – but it's easy enough to see the sunlight glinting on the glasses. Gosh, what cheek!'

'Cheek!' said George, her face crimson with rage. 'It's a lot more than cheek! How *dare* people go on my island and use it to spy on people on the beach? Let's spy on *them*! Let's get our own field-glasses and look through them. We'll see who it is, then!'

'I'll get them,' said Dick and ran off to Kirrin Cottage. He felt worried. It seemed a strange thing to do – to spy on people sitting on the beach round the bay, using binoculars on Kirrin Island. What was the reason?

He came back with the binoculars, and handed them to Julian. 'I think they're gone now, whoever it was,' said Julian. 'I don't mean gone off the island, but gone somewhere else on it. We can't see the glint of the sun on their glasses any more.'

'Well, buck up and see if you can spy anyone through *our* glasses,' said George, impatiently.

Julian adjusted them, and gazed through them earnestly. The island seemed very near indeed when seen through the powerful glasses. Everyone watched him anxiously.

'See anyone?' asked Dick.

'Not a soul,' said Julian, disappointed. He handed the glasses to the impatient George, who put them to her eyes at once. 'Blow!' she said. 'There's not a thing to be seen, not a thing. Whoever it was has gone into hiding somewhere. If it's trippers having a picnic there I'll be absolutely furious. If we see smoke rising we'll know it *is* trippers!'

But no smoke arose. Dick had a turn at looking through the glasses, and he looked puzzled. He took them down from his eyes and turned to the others.

'We ought to be able to see the rabbits running

about,' he said. 'But I can't see a single one. Did either of you, Julian and George?'

'Well – now I come to think of it – no, I didn't,' said Julian, and George said the same.

'They were frightened by whoever was there, of course,' said Dick. 'I suppose it will be all right to take Lesley with us when we go to the island this afternoon? I mean – it's just a bit *odd* that anyone should be using the island to spy from.'

'Yes. I see what you mean,' said Julian. 'If it occurred to the kidnappers, whoever they are, that Berta *might* be down here with us, it would be quite a good idea on their part to land on the island and use it as a place from which to spy on the beach. They would guess we would come down to bathe every day.'

'Yes. And they would see five children instead of four and would begin to make enquiries about the fifth!' said Dick. 'They would hope actually to *see* Berta on the beach – they've probably got a photograph of her – and they would be looking for a girl with long wavy hair.'

'And there isn't one!' said Anne. 'Mine's not wavy and it's not right down to my shoulders as Lesley's was. How muddled they would be!'

'There's one thing that would tell them that Berta was here though,' said Julian, suddenly. He pointed to Sally.

'Good gracious, yes!' said Dick. 'Sally would give the game away all right! Whew! We'll have to think about all this!'

11 On Kirrin Island again

George wanted to get her boat and go across to the island immediately. She was so furious at the thought of anyone else being there without permission that all she wanted to do was to chase them away.

But Julian said no. 'For one thing the boat won't be ready till two,' he said. 'For another thing we've got to consider whether it's a sensible thing to do, to go to the island *if* possible kidnappers are here, on the lookout for Berta – Lesley, I mean.'

'We could go without her,' said George. 'We could leave her safely with Joanna.'

'That would be a foolish thing to do,' said Dick. 'Anyone watching us coming across in the boat would see that one of the five was missing, and would guess at once it was Berta. If we go, *all* of us must go.'

'Actually I think it might be a good thing to do,' said Julian. 'Carry the war right into the enemy's camp, so to speak – if there *are* enemies! It would be a most useful thing if we could see what they are like and give a description to the police. I rather vote we go.'

'Oh *yes*!' said Dick. 'Anyway, we'll have Tim with us. He can deal with any bad behaviour on the part of the intruders!'

'I don't really think it's anybody but trippers,' said Julian. 'I think we're making too much of the whole thing just because someone gazed at the beach through glasses!'

'Remember that I think I saw a light on the island

last night,' Anne reminded him.

'Yes, I'd forgotten that,' said Julian, looking at his watch. 'It's almost lunch-time. Let's go and have something to eat, and then fetch the boat. James is working on it now. We'll give him a shout to see if it will be ready at two.'

James was hailed, and he shouted back. 'Yes! Be ready sharp at two o'clock, if you want her. I've done one or two little jobs on her besides the rowlock.'

'That's good,' said Dick, and they walked back to Kirrin Cottage. 'Well, we'll soon find out who's on your island, George – and if they are obstinate about leaving, we'll have a little fun with Timmy! He can round them up all right, can't you, Tim!'

'So could Sally,' said Berta. 'Sally's teeth aren't very big, but they're sharp. She once went for a man who accidentally pushed into me, and you should have seen the nips she gave him, all down his leg!'

'Yes. Sally would come in useful,' said Dick. George looked rather scornful. 'That silly little poodle!' she thought. 'A fat lot of good *she* would be! Timmy's worth a hundred of her!'

Joanna had a fine lunch ready for them – ham and salad and new potatoes piled high in a big dish. There were firm red tomatoes from the greenhouse, and lettuces with enormous yellow-green hearts, crisp radishes, and a whole cucumber ready for anyone to cut as they liked. Slices of hard-boiled egg were mixed in with the salad, and Joanna had put in tiny boiled carrots and peas as well.

'What a salad!' said Dick. 'Fit for a king!'

'And big enough for *several* kings!' said Anne. 'How many potatoes, Ju? Small or large ones?'

Julian looked at the piled-up dish. 'Ha – I can really go for these potatoes!' he said. 'I'll have three large and four small.'

'What's for pudding?' asked Berta. 'I like this kind of salad so much that I might not have room for a stodgy sort of pudding.'

'It's fresh raspberries from the garden, sugar and home-made ice-cream,' said Joanna. 'I didn't think you'd want a hot pudding. My sister came to see me this morning, so I got her to pick the raspberries for me.'

'I can't think of a nicer meal than this,' said Berta, helping herself to the salad. 'I really can't. I like your meals better than the ones we have at home in America.'

'We'll turn you into a proper little English boy before you know where you are!' said Dick.

They told Joanna about what they had seen that morning on the island. She took a grave view of it at once.

'Now you know what your aunt said, Julian,' she said. 'The police have got to have a report of anything suspicious. You'd better ring them up.'

'I will when we've been over to the island and back,' said Julian. 'I don't want to look an ass, Joanna. If it's only harmless trippers who don't know any better there's no need to bother the police. I *promise* to ring the police if we find anything suspicious.'

'I think you ought to ring them *now*,' said Joanna. 'And what's more I don't think you ought to go over to the island if you're suspicious of the people there.'

'We'll have Timmy with us,' said Dick. 'Don't worry.'

'And Sally too,' added Berta at once.

Joanna said no more, but went out to get the raspberries and ice-cream, looking worried. She brought in an enormous glass dish of fresh red raspberries and another dish of creamy-looking ice-cream blocks from the refrigerator.

A sigh of admiration went up from everyone. 'Who could want anything better?' said Dick. 'And that ice-cream – how do you get it like that, Joanna – not too frozen and not too melty? Just how I like it. I do hope some American doesn't get hold of you and whisk you away across the ocean – you're worth your weight in gold!'

Joanna laughed. 'You say such extravagant things, Dick – and all because of an ordinary dish like raspberries and ice-cream. Get along with you! Lesley will tell you there's nothing clever about raspberries and cream.'

'I agree with every word the others say,' said Berta fervently. 'You're wunnerful, you're a honey, you're . . .'

But Joanna had run out of the room, laughing, very pleased. She didn't mind what she did for children like these!

After they had finished lunch, they went down to the beach. James was still with the boat.

'She's finished!' he called. 'You going out in her now? I'll give you a hand down with her, then.'

Soon all five children and the dogs as well were in George's boat. The boys took the oars and began to pull hard towards the island. Timmy stood at the prow as he loved to do, fore-paws on the edge of the boat, looking out across the water.

'He fancies himself as a figurehead,' said Dick. 'Ah, here comes Sally – she wants to be one too. Mind you don't fall overboard, Sally, and get your pretty feet wet. You'll have to learn to swim if you do!'

Sally stood close beside Timmy, and both dogs looked eagerly towards the island – Timmy because he knew there were hundreds of rabbits there, and Sally because for her it was still quite an adventure to go out in a boat like this.

Berta, too, gazed eagerly at the little island as they drew near. She had heard so many tales about it now! She looked especially at the old castle rising up from it. It was in ruins, and Berta thought it must be very old indeed. Like so many Americans, she loved old buildings and old customs. How lucky George was to own an island like this!

Rocks guarded the island, and the sea ran strongly over them, sending up spray and foam.

'How ever are we going to get safely to the shore of the island?' said Berta, rather alarmed at the array of fierce-looking rocks that guarded it.

'There's a little cove we always use,' said George. She was at the tiller, and she steered the boat cleverly in and out of the rocks.

They rounded a low wall of very sharp rocks and Berta suddenly saw the little cove.

'Oh – is that the cove you mean?' she said. 'Why, it's like a little harbour going right up to that stretch of sand!'

There was a smooth inlet of water running between rocks, making a natural little harbour, as Berta said. The boat slid smoothly into the inlet and up to the beach of sand.

Dick leapt out and pulled it up the shore. 'She's safe here,' he told Berta. 'Welcome to Kirrin Island!'

Berta laughed. She felt very happy. What a truly wonderful place to come to!

George led the way up the sandy beach to the rocks behind, and they climbed over them. They stopped at the top, and Berta exclaimed in amazement.

'Rabbits! Thousand of them! Simply thousands. My, my, I never saw such tame ones in my life. Will they let me pick them up?'

'No,' said George. 'They're not as tame as that! They'll run away when we go near – but they will

probably not go into their holes. They know us –
we've so often been here.'

Sally the poodle was amazed at the rabbits. She
couldn't believe her eyes. She stood close beside Berta,
staring at the scuttling rabbits, her nose twitching as
she tried to get their smell. She simply couldn't understand why Timmy didn't run at them.

Timmy stood quite still beside George, his tail
down, looking very mournful. A visit to Kirrin Island
was not such a pleasure to him as to the children,
because he wasn't allowed to hunt the rabbits. *What* a
waste of rabbits!

'Poor old Tim! Look at him!' said Julian. 'He looks
the picture of misery. Look at Sally, too – she's
longing to go after the rabbits, but she doesn't think
it's good manners to chase them till Timmy does!'

Good manners or not, little Sally could bear it no
longer! She suddenly made a dart at a rabbit who had
come temptingly near, and it leapt into the air in
fright.

'Sally!' called George, in a most peremptory manner. 'NO! You're not to chase my rabbits! Tim – go
and fetch her here!'

Timmy went off to Sally and gave a tiny little
growl. Sally looked at him in amazement. Could her
friend Timmy *really* be growling at her? Timmy began
to push himself against her and she found herself
shepherded over to George.

'Good dog, Timmy,' said George, pleased to have
shown everyone how obedient he was. 'Sally, you
mustn't chase these rabbits, because they are too
tame! They haven't learnt to run away properly yet,
because not many people come here and frighten
them.'

'Whoever was here this morning scared them all
right,' said Julian, remembering. 'Gosh, don't let's

forget there may be people here. Well – I can't see anyone so far!'

They went cautiously forward, towards the old castle, Timmy running ahead. Then Julian stopped and pointed to the ground.

'Cigarette ends – look! Fresh ones, too. There *are* people here, that's certain. Walk ahead of us, Tim.'

But at that moment there came the sound that Anne had heard the night before – the sound of a motor-boat's engine. R-r-r-r-r-r-r!

'They're escaping!' cried Dick. 'Quick, run to the other side of the island! We may see them then!'

12   *Very suspicious*

The children, with the two dogs barking excitedly, ran to the other, seaward side of the island. Great rocks lay out there, and the sea splashed over them.

'There it is – a motorboat!' cried Dick. They all stood and watched the boat riding over the sea at a very fast speed.

'Where are the glasses – did we bring them with us?' said Julian. 'I'd like to focus them on the boat and see if I can read the name – or even see the men in it!'

But the glasses had been left behind at Kirrin Cottage – what a pity!

'They must have anchored their motorboat out there, and somehow clambered inshore over the rocks,' said George. 'It's a dangerous thing to do if you don't know the best way.'

'Yes – and if they came last night, as I think they must have done, because I'm sure now it was the engine of the motorboat that I heard,' said Anne, 'if they came last night, they must have clambered to the shore in the dark. I wonder they managed it!'

'It must have been the light of a lantern or a torch you saw on the island in the night,' said Julian. 'They probably didn't want to be seen arriving on the island, and that's why they went to the other side, the seaward side. I wonder if they *were* men spying to find out if Berta is with us or not.'

'Let's snoop around a bit more and see if we can find

anything else,' said Anne. 'The motorboat is almost out of sight now.'

They went back to the other side of the island. Berta looked with awe at the old castle in the middle. Jackdaws circled round a tower, calling loudly. 'Chack-chack-chack!'

'Once upon a time my castle had strong walls all round it,' said George. 'And there were two great towers. One's almost in ruins, as you can see, but the other is fairly good. Come right into the castle.'

Berta followed the others in, struck dumb with awe. To think that this island, and this wonderful old ruined castle, belonged to George! How very, very lucky she was!

She went through a great doorway, and found herself in a dark room, with stone walls enclosing it. Two narrow, slit-like windows brought in all the light there was.

'It's strange and old and mysterious,' said Berta, half to herself. 'It's asleep and dreaming of the old days when people lived here. It doesn't like us being here!'

'Wake up!' said Dick. 'You look quite dopey!' Berta shook herself and looked round again. Then she went on through the castle and looked at other rooms, some without roofs, some without one or two of their walls.

'It's a honey of a castle!' she said to George. 'A real honey. Wunnerful. WonDERful.'

They wandered all round, showing the awe-struck Berta everything. 'We'll show you the dungeons too,' said George, very pleased to be impressing Berta so much.

'Dungeons! You've got dungeons too – oh, of course, you told me about them,' said Berta. '*Dungeons!* You don't say! My my, I'll never forget this afternoon.'

As they walked over the old courtyard Timmy

suddenly growled and stood still, his tail down, the hackles on his neck rising. Everyone automatically stood still too.

'What is it, Tim?' asked George, in a whisper. Timmy's nose was pointing towards the little harbour where they had left their boat.

'There must be someone there,' said Dick. 'Don't say they're going off with our boat!'

George gave a scream. Her boat! Her precious boat! She set off at top speed with Timmy bounding in front.

'Come back, George – there may be danger!' shouted Julian, but George didn't listen. She ran over the rocks that led down to the little harbour beach, and then stopped still in surprise.

Two policemen were walking up the sandy beach! Their boat was drawn up beside George's. They saluted her and grinned.

'Afternoon, George!'

'What are you doing on my island?' demanded George, recognising them. 'Why have you come here?'

'Someone reported suspicious people on the island,' said the first policeman.

'*Who* did?' said George. 'Nobody knew about it but us!'

'I bet I know who reported it,' said Dick suddenly. 'Joanna did! She didn't like us going off by ourselves; she said we ought to telephone the police.'

'That's right,' said the policeman. 'So we came to see for ourselves. Found anyone?'

Julian took command then, and related how they had first seen the cigarette ends, and then heard the motorboat starting up, and had gone to see it roaring away from the island.

'Ah,' said the policeman, profoundly. 'Ah!'

'What do you mean – "AH"?' asked Dick.

'Fred here heard a motorboat somewhere in the bay in the night,' said the first man. 'What was it doing there, I'd like to know?'

'So would we,' said Julian. '*We* saw someone on the island looking through binoculars at the beach this morning.'

This brought forth two more 'Ahs', and the police-men exchanged glances.

'Good thing you've got a couple of dogs with you,' said the one called Fred. 'Well – we'll just have a bit of a look round, and then we'll go back on our beats again. And mind you ring us up next time anything turns up, George, see?'

Off they went together, looking closely at the ground. They found the cigarette ends and picked them up. Then on they went again.

'Let's go back,' said George, in a low voice. 'It spoils things if other people are on the island. I don't want to have a picnic here now. We'll go off in the boat somewhere and have a picnic tea in a cove.'

So they dragged the boat down to the water and jumped in. Sally was very pleased to be back in the boat and ran from end to end wagging her stiff tail in delight. Timmy followed her up and down and got in everyone's way.

'How can I row if you keep on jumping over me, Timmy?' complained Dick. 'Sally, you're just as bad. Berta, are you all right? You look a bit green?'

'It's only excitement and the bumpy bit past the rocks,' said Berta, anxious not to appear seasick in front of the others. 'I'll be all right as soon as we get on to calm waters.'

But she wasn't, so it was regretfully decided that they must row to the shore. They had a lazy tea on the beach, and Berta recovered enough to join in heartily.

'Anyone got room for an ice-cream?' asked Anne. 'Because if so I'll stroll down to the shops and get some. I want to buy a new pair of shoe-laces too. One of mine broke this morning.'

Everyone appeared to have room for an ice-cream, so Anne set off with Sally, who wanted to come with her. She went to the draper's and got the laces, and then went to the tea-shop that sold ices.

'Seven, please,' she said. The girl in the shop smiled.

'Seven! You used to ask for five.'

'Yes, I know. But we've got someone staying with us – and another dog,' explained Anne. 'And both dogs like ice-creams.'

'That reminds me – someone was in my shop yesterday asking about your uncle,' said the girl. 'He said he knew him. He wanted to know how many children were staying at Kirrin Cottage, and I thought only the four of you were there – and Timmy, of course. He seemed surprised, and said, surely there was another girl?'

'Good gracious!' said Anne, startled. 'Did he really? How inquisitive! What did you say then?'

'I just said there were two boys and a girl, and a girl who liked to dress as a boy,' said the girl.

Anne was glad to think the shop-girl hadn't known about Berta. 'What was the man like?' she asked.

'Quite ordinary,' said the girl, trying to remember. 'He wore dark glasses like so many visitors do in the bright sun. I noticed he had a large gold ring on his finger when he paid my bill. That's all I can remember.'

'Well, if anyone else asks you about us, just say we've got a friend staying with us called Lesley,' said Anne. 'Goodbye.'

She went off at top speed, anxious to tell the others. The man in the tea-shop must have been one of those who had gone to the island to watch the beach – he might have been staring at the five of them as they had played together. He must be one of the men now in the motorboat. Anne didn't like it, and it made her feel very uneasy.

She told the others what the shop-girl had said as they sat in the sand and ate their ice-creams. Timmy gobbled his almost at once, and sat patiently watching Sally deal with hers, hoping that she would leave some.

All the four listened intently to Anne's little story. 'That settles it,' said Dick. 'Those men are certainly snooping round trying to find out if Lesley is here.'

'They are getting uncomfortably close,' said Julian.

'Still, your uncle and aunt come back tomorrow,' said Berta. 'We'll tell them, and maybe they'll have some good plan.'

'I hope those men don't know that they are away,' said Dick, uneasily. 'I think we'll have to keep a pretty close watch from now on. I wonder if Berta ought to stay on here with us.'

'See what Father says tomorrow,' said George. So it was decided that nothing should be done except to keep a sharp look-out until George's parents came back. They all went back rather soberly to Kirrin Cottage and told Joanna what had happened on the island.

'You telephoned the police, Joanna!' said Dick, shaking his finger at her.

'I did. And I was right to,' said Joanna. 'And what's more, Lesley's bed is going to be moved away from the window tonight *and* the window's going to be fastened even if we melt, *and* the door will be locked.'

'I'll lend you Timmy, too, if you like,' said George. 'He can sleep in the room with Sally. You ought to be safe then!'

She really only meant it as a joke, but to her surprise Joanna accepted at once. 'Thank you,' she said. 'I'd be glad of Timmy. I feel all of a dither, left on my own like this, and kidnappers closing in on us!'

Julian laughed. 'Oh, it's not so bad as that, Joanna. Only one more night and Uncle Quentin and Aunt Fanny will be back.'

'Oh – I quite forgot to tell you,' said Joanna. 'A letter's arrived. They're staying away a whole week! That's why I feel so scared. A week – well, a lot can happen in a week!'

13 A horrid shock

Julian was not very happy to hear that his aunt and uncle were staying away for a week. He picked up the letter. It was addressed to George, but Joanna had opened it.

'Not returning for a week,' it said. 'Complications have arisen. Hope all goes well. Love from Mother.'

There was no address. How annoying! Now Julian couldn't even let them *know* that he was feeling uneasy. He made up his mind to guard Berta every minute! Thank goodness they had Timmy. Nobody would dare to do any kidnapping under Timmy's eye!

He thought it was a good idea to put Timmy in Joanna's room that night with Berta. In fact, if George would agree, it would be best to do that each night. He thought it would not be wise to ask George now, though, because he could see that she was half sorry she had made the offer to Joanna!

Julian was quite fussy that evening. He insisted on the blinds being drawn when they sat down to play cards after their supper. He would not let Berta take Sally out for a run, but took her himself, watching for any strange person as he went down the lane.

'You're making me feel quite scared!' said Anne with a laugh. 'Oh Ju, it's so hot in this room. Do, do let's have the blind up for a few minutes and let some air in. I shall begin to sizzle if we don't. Timmy would soon growl if there was anyone outside.'

'All right,' said Julian and drew up the blind. It was

dark outside now, and the light streamed out.

'That's better,' said Anne, mopping her wet fore-head. 'Now, whose turn is it? Yours, George.'

They sat round the table, playing. Julian and Berta sat side by side, as Julian was helping her in a new game of cards. She looked exactly like a very earnest little boy, with her straight close-cut fair hair. George sat opposite the window with Dick on one side of her and Anne on the other.

'Your turn, Dick,' said George. 'Do buck up, you're slow tonight.' She sat and waited, looking out of the window into the darkness.

Then suddenly she slammed down her cards and leapt up, shouting. Everyone jumped almost out of their skins.

'What is it, what is it, George?' cried Julian.

'Out there – look – a face! I saw a face peeping in at us – the light of the window just caught it! Timmy, Timmy! Quick, go after him!'

But Timmy wasn't there! Nor was Sally. George called frantically again. 'TIMMY! Come here, quickly. Oh, blow him, that fellow will get away. TIM!'

Timmy came bounding up the hall and into the sitting-room, barking. Sally followed behind.

'Where were you! Idiot!' cried George furiously. 'Jump out of the window – go on – chase him, find him!'

Timmy leapt out of the window and Sally tried to do the same, but couldn't. She barked and yelped, trying again and again to jump out. Joanna came running in, panic-stricken, wondering what was happening.

'*Listen*,' said Julian, suddenly. 'Shut up, Sally. *Listen!*'

They were all suddenly quiet, Sally too. There was

the sound of a car being revved up down the lane, and then the sound died down as the car sped away.

'He's got away, whoever he was,' said Dick, and sat down suddenly. 'Gosh, I feel as if I'd been running a mile. You nearly scared the life out of me when you slammed down your cards like that, George, and yelled in my ear.'

Timmy leapt in at the window at that moment and Dick almost jumped out of his skin again. So did everyone else, including Sally, who fled behind the sofa in panic.

'*What's* all this about?' said Joanna, quite fiercely. 'Really!'

George was in a tearing rage – with Timmy of all things! She shouted at the surprised dog and he put his tail down at once.

'Where were you? Why did you slink out of the room into the kitchen? How dare you leave me and go off like that? Just when we needed you! I'm ashamed of you, Timmy – you could have caught that fellow easily!'

'Oh don't,' said Berta, almost in tears. 'Poor Timmy! Don't, George!'

Then George turned on Berta. 'You just let me scold my own dog if he needs it! And you go and scold yours too. I bet Timmy followed your horrid little woolly pet out into the kitchen – it was *her* fault, not his!'

'Shut up, George,' said Julian. 'Your temper gets us nowhere. Calm down and let's hear what you saw. CALM DOWN, I say.'

George stared at him, about to retort with something defiant. Then Timmy gave a small whimper – his heart was almost broken to hear George – George, his beloved mistress – rave at him in such anger. He had no idea what he had done to displease her.

The whimper brought George to her senses. 'Oh

Timmy!' she said, and knelt down and flung her arms round his neck. 'I didn't mean to shout at you. I was so angry because we missed our chance of getting that man who was peeping in at us. Oh Timmy, it's all right, it really is.'

Timmy was extremely glad to hear it. He licked George lavishly, and then lay down by her very soberly. He wished he knew what all the excitement was about.

So did Joanna. She thumped on the table to get everyone's attention, and at last got Julian to explain everything to her. She stared out of the window, half-thinking that she could see faces in the darkness outside. She drew the blind down sharply.

'We'll go to bed,' she said. 'All of us. I don't like this. I shall ring up the police and warn them. Lesley, you come with me straight away now.'

'I think perhaps you're right, Joanna,' said Julian. 'I'll lock up everywhere. Come on, girls.'

Timmy was astonished and upset to find himself handed over to Joanna and Berta. Was George still cross with him then? It was a very, very long time since he had slept away from her at night. He cheered up a little when he saw that Sally was going to be with him, and trotted rather mournfully up the attic stairs to Joanna's room.

Joanna soon got Berta into bed, and then undressed herself. She fastened the window and locked the door. She gave Timmy a rug in a corner, and Sally jumped up on Berta's bed as usual.

'Now we ought to be quite safe!' said Joanna, and settled creakingly into her bed.

On the floor below the two boys followed the same procedure, and so did Anne and George. Doors were locked and windows fastened, though it was a hot night and they were all sure they would be melted by

the morning. George couldn't bear to think of Timmy
with Berta and Joanna – especially as she had been so
very cross with him. She lay in bed, full of remorse.
Dear, kind, faithful Timmy – how *could* she have
shouted at him like that?'

'Do you suppose Timmy is feeling very upset?' she
said, when she and Anne were in bed.

'A bit, perhaps,' said Anne. 'But dogs are very
forgiving.'

'I know. That somehow makes it worse,' said
George.

'Well, you really *shouldn't* get into such tempers,'
said Anne, seizing the opportunity to tell George a few
home truths. 'I thought you were getting over the
tantrums you used to have. But these hols you've been
pretty bad. Because of Berta, I suppose.'

'I wish I could go up and say goodnight to Timmy,'
George began again, after a few minutes' silence.

'Oh for goodness sake, George!' said Anne, sleepily. 'Do be sensible. You *can't* go and bang on Joanna's
door and ask for Timmy – you'd scare them to
death!'

Anne fell asleep, but George didn't. Then suddenly
she heard the sound of a door being unlocked, and sat
up. It sounded as if it came from the attic. Was it
Joanna unlocking her door? What did she want?

A cautious little knock came at George's door. 'Who
is it?' said George.

'Me. Joanna,' said Joanna's voice. 'I've brought
Sally down, George. Timmy keeps trying to get up on
Berta's bed to be with Sally, and she simply *can't* go to
sleep, her camp-bed is too small to hold all three of
them. So will you have Sally, please?'

'Oh blow!' said George, and went to open her door.
'How's Timmy?' she said, in a low voice.

'All right,' said Joanna. 'He'll be annoyed I've taken

Sally away. I'm glad to have him up there tonight with all these goings on!'

'Is he – is he happy, Joanna?' asked George, but Joanna had turned away and didn't hear. George sighed. *Why* had she offered to let Joanna and Berta have Timmy tonight of all nights, when she had scolded him so unfairly? Now she had to have this silly little Sally instead!

Sally whimpered. She didn't like being away from Berta, and she was not fond of George. She wriggled out of George's arms and ran round the room, still whimpering.

Anne woke up with a jump. 'Whatever's going on?' she said. 'Why – it's Sally in the room! How did *she* get here?'

George told her, sounding very cross. 'Well, I hope she'll settle down,' said Anne. 'I don't want her to whimper and run round the bedroom all night long.'

But Sally wouldn't settle down. Her whimpering became louder, and when she took a flying jump on to George's bed and landed right on George's middle, the girl had had enough of it. She sat up and spoke in a fierce whisper.

'You little idiot! I'm jolly well going to take you downstairs and put you into Timmy's kennel!'

'Good idea,' said Anne, sleepily. George picked up the lively little poodle and went out of the room, shutting the door softly. Anne promptly went to sleep again.

George crept down the stairs and went to the garden door. She undid it and walked out in dressing-gown and pyjamas, her curly hair all tousled, carrying the whimpering little dog.

Suddenly she felt Sally stiffen in her arms, and growl. Grrrrrrr! George stood quite still. What had Sally heard?

Then things happened very suddenly indeed. A torch was flashed in her face, and before she could cry out, a cloth was thrown over her head so that she could not make a sound.

'This is the one!' said a low voice. 'The one with curly hair! And this is her dog, the poodle. Put him in that kennel, quick, before he barks the place down.'

Sally, too scared even to growl, was pushed into the kennel and the door shut on her. George, struggling and trying vainly to call out, was lifted off her feet and carried swiftly down to the front gate.

The garden door swung creaking to and fro in the night wind. Sally whimpered in her kennel. But no one heard either door or dog. Everyone in Kirrin Cottage was sound asleep!

14 Where is George?

Next morning, about half past seven, Joanna went downstairs as usual. Berta was awake and decided to fetch Sally from George's bedroom. She put on her dressing-gown and padded downstairs with Timmy behind her, to George's room on the foor below. The door was shut, and she knocked gently.

'Come in,' said Anne's sleepy voice. 'Oh, it's you, Berta.'

'Yes. I've come for Sally,' said Berta. 'Hallo – where's George?'

Anne looked at the empty bed beside hers. 'I don't know. The last thing I heard of her was in the middle of the night when we got cross because Sally wouldn't settle down, and George said she would take her down to the kennel.'

'Oh. Well, probably George has gone down to fetch her back,' said Berta. 'I'll go up and dress. It's a heavenly morning again. Are you going to bathe before breakfast, because if so I'll just put on my swimsuit.'

'Yes. I think we might today – we're nice and early,' said Anne, scrambling out of bed. 'Go and wake the boys. Timmy, go down and find George.'

Dick and Julian were awake, and quite ready for a before-breakfast bathe. Anne joined them as they went downstairs. Berta had already gone down and had discovered Sally in the kennel, most excited to see her. She pranced round barking happily.

Timmy came up to the children, looking puzzled. He had hunted everywhere for George and hadn't found her. 'Woof,' he said to Anne. 'Woof, woof!' It was just as if he were saying, 'Please, where is George?'

'Haven't you found George yet?' said Anne in surprise. She called to Joanna. 'Joanna, where's George? Has she gone down to bathe already?'

'I haven't seen her,' said Joanna. 'But I expect she has because the garden door was open when I came down, and I guessed one of you had gone for an early bathe.'

'Well, George must be down on the beach, then,' said Anne, feeling rather puzzled. Why hadn't George woken her and told her to come too?

Soon all four were on the beach with the two dogs, Sally very happy to be with Berta again, and Timmy very downcast and puzzled. He stood staring up the beach and down, looking quite lost.

'I can't see George anywhere,' said Dick, suddenly feeling scared. 'She's not in the sea.'

They all gazed over the water, but no one was bathing that morning. Anne turned to Julian in sudden panic.

'Ju! Where is she?'

'I wish I knew,' said Julian, anxiously. 'She's not here. And she hasn't gone out in her boat – it's over there. Let's go back to the house.'

'I don't think George would have gone for an early bathe without telling me,' said Anne. 'And I also think I would surely have woken up just for a moment when she came back after taking Sally down – oh Julian, I think something happened when she went downstairs with Sally late last night!'

'I've been thinking that too,' said Julian soberly. 'We know that there was someone about last night,

because George saw a face outside the window. Let's
go back to the house and see if we can spot anything to
help us near the garden door or the kennel.'

They went back, looking very anxious. As soon as
they began to look about near the kennel, Anne gave
an exclamation and bent down. She picked up something and held it out to the others without a word.

'What is it – gosh, it's the girdle off George's
dressing-gown!' said Dick, startled. 'That proves it!
George was caught when she came down to put Sally
into her kennel!'

'They must have thought she was *me*,' said Berta, in
tears. 'You see – she was carrying Sally and they know
Sally belongs to me – and she has short hair too and
dresses like a boy in the daytime.'

'That's it!' said Julian. 'Actually you *look* like a boy
in your boy's things, but George doesn't – and the
kidnappers are looking for a girl dressed as a boy – and
George fitted the bill nicely, especially as she had the
poodle with her. She's been kidnapped!'

'And will my father get the usual note to say his
daughter will not be harmed if he does what the
kidnappers want, and hands over this new secret?' said
Berta.

'Sure to,' said Julian.

'What will they say when they know they've got
George, not me?' asked Berta.

'Well . . .' said Julian, considering. 'I really don't
know. They might try the same thing with Uncle
Quentin, but of course, he hasn't got the figures they
want.'

'What about *Berta* now?' asked Dick. 'Once those
men find they've got the wrong girl, they'll be after
Berta in a trice!'

'George won't tell them,' said Anne, at once. 'She'll
know that Berta would be in immediate danger if she

did tell them – so she'll say nothing as long as she can.'

'Would she really?' said Berta, wonderingly. 'She's brave, isn't she? She could get herself set free at once if she said she wasn't me, and proved it. Gee, she's wunnerful if she could do a thing like that!'

'George is brave all right,' said Dick. 'As brave as anything when she's in a fix! Julian, let's go and tell Joanna. We've GOT to make up our minds what we are going to do about this – and also, we *must* safeguard Berta somehow. She can't possibly wander round with us any more.'

Berta all at once began to feel scared. George's sudden disappearance had brought home to her the very real danger she was in. She had not really believed in it before. She looked over her shoulder and all round and about as if she expected someone to pounce on her.

'It's all right, Berta – there's no one here at present!' said Dick, comfortingly. 'But you'd better get indoors, all the same. I don't *think* George would give away the fact that she wasn't you, but the men might find out some other way – and back they would come, hotfoot!'

Berta raced indoors as if someone was chasing her! Julian shut and locked the garden door and called Joanna.

They had a very serious conference indeed. Joanna was horrified. She wept when she heard that George must have been kidnapped in the middle of the night. She wiped her eyes with her apron.

'I *said* we must lock the doors and the windows, I *said* we must tell the police – and then George has to go down all by herself into the garden!' she said. 'If only she hadn't had the poodle with her! No wonder they thought she was Berta, with Sally in her arms.'

'Listen, Joanna,' said Julian. 'There are a lot of

things to do. First we must tell the police. Then somehow we must contact Aunt Fanny and Uncle Quentin – it's so like them not to give us an address! Then we must most certainly decide about Berta. She must be well hidden away somewhere.'

'Yes. That's certain,' said Joanna wiping her eyes again. She sat and thought for a minute, and then her face lightened.

'I know where we could hide her!' she said. 'You remember Jo – the little traveller girl you've had one or two adventures with?'

'Yes,' said Julian. 'She lives with your cousin now, doesn't she?'

'She does,' said Joanna. 'And my cousin would have Berta straight away if she knew about this. She lives in a quiet little village where nothing ever happens, and nobody would think anything of my cousin having a child to stay with Jo. She often does.'

'It really seems an idea,' said Dick. 'Doesn't it, Julian? We've simply *got* to get Berta away at once. We could trust Jo to look after her, too – Jo's as sharp as a packet of needles!'

'The police would know, too,' said Julian, 'and would keep an eye on her as well. Joanna, can you ring up and get a taxi and take Berta now, this very minute?'

'It'll be a surprise for my cousin, my arriving this time of the morning,' said Joanna, standing up and taking off her apron, 'but she's quick on the uptake, and she'll do it, I know. Lesley, get a few things together – nothing posh, mind, like your silver hairbrush.'

Berta looked extremely scared by now, and was inclined to refuse to go. Julian put his arm round her.

'Look,' he said, 'I bet George is holding her tongue so that we can get you away in safety before the men trumble to the fact that they've got the wrong boy – so you can play up, too, can't you, and be brave?'

'Yes,' said Berta, looking up at Julian's kind, serious face. 'I'll do what you say – but what's this Jo like? Joanna said she was a little traveller girl. I might not like her.'

'You'll like this one all right,' said Julian. 'She's a pickle and a scamp and a scallywag – but her heart's in the right place – isn't it, Joanna?'

Joanna nodded. She had always been fond of the reckless, cheeky little Jo, and it was she who had found a home for her when Jo's father had had to go to prison. 'Come on, Lesley,' she said. 'We must hurry. Julian, is she to go as a girl or a boy now – we've got to decide that too.'

'A girl, please, please, a girl!' said Berta, at once.

Julian considered. 'Yes, I think you're right,' he said. 'You'd better be a girl now – but for goodness sake don't call yourself Berta yet.'

'She can be Jane,' said Joanna, firmly. 'That's a nice name, but quite ordinary enough for nobody to notice. Berta is too noticeable a name. Come along, now – we'll have to pick out your simplest clothes!'

'Now I'll ring up the police,' said Julian, 'and also ring for a taxi.'

'No, don't get a taxi for us,' said Joanna. 'I don't want to arrive at my cousin's little cottage in a taxi, and make everyone stare! Jane and I will catch the market bus and people will think I'm going off to market. We can get another bus there, that will take us almost all the way to my cousin's. We've only to walk down the lane then.'

'Good idea,' said Julian, and went to the telephone. He got hold of the police sergeant, and told his tale. The man showed not the least excitement, but took down quickly all that Julian told him. 'I'll be up in ten minutes,' he said. 'Wait in till I come.'

Julian put down the receiver. Dick and Anne were watching him with troubled eyes. What was happening to George? Was she frightened – or furious – or perhaps hurt?

Timmy was absolutely miserable. He knew by now that something had happened to George. He had gone a dozen times to the place where her dressing-gown girdle had been found, and had sniffed round disconsolately.

Sally knew he was unhappy and trotted after him soberly. When he lay down she lay down beside him. When he got up, she got up too. It would have been amusing to watch if anyone had felt like being amused. But nobody felt that way!

Footsteps came up the path. 'The police!' said Julian. 'They've not been long!'

15   Discoveries in the wood

The sergeant had come and also a constable. Anne felt comforted when she saw the big, solid, responsible-looking men. Julian took them into the sitting-room, and began to tell all that had happened.

In the middle of it there came the sound of footsteps racing down the stairs, and up the hall. 'We're just off!' shouted Joanna's voice. 'Can't stop to say goodbye, or we shall miss the bus!'

Down the garden path rushed Joanna, carrying a small suitcase of her own, which she had lent Berta, because Berta's was too grand. In it she had packed the very simplest of Berta's clothes, but secretly she had thought that she would tell her cousin to dress Berta in some of Jo's things.

Berta ran behind her – a different Berta now, dressed in a frock instead of jeans and jersey. She waved to the others as she went, trying to smile.

'Good old Berta!' said Dick. 'She's got quite a lot in her, that kid.'

'In fact, she's quite a honey!' said Julian, trying to make Anne smile.

'What's all that?' said the sergeant, in surprise, nodding his head towards the front path, down which Joanna and Berta had just rushed.

Julian explained. The sergeant frowned. 'You shouldn't have arranged about that till you'd consulted us,' he said. Julian was quite taken aback.

'Well, you see,' he said, 'it seemed to me that I must

get Berta out of the house and hidden away at once in case the kidnappers realised quickly that they'd got the wrong girl.'

'That's so,' said the sergeant. 'Still, you *should* have consulted us. It seems quite a good idea to put her in that quiet village, with Jo to see to her – she's sharp, that Jo. I wouldn't put it past her to hoodwink the kidnappers any day! But this is a very serious business, you realise, Julian – it can't be dealt with by children.'

'Can you get George back?' asked Anne, breaking in with the question she had been longing to ask ever since the police came.

'Maybe,' said the sergeant. 'Now I'll get in touch with your aunt and uncle, Julian, and with Mr Elbur Wright, and . . .'

The telephone rang just then and Anne answered it. 'It's for you, Sergeant,' she said, and he took the receiver from her.

'Ha. Hm. Just so. Yes, yes. Right. Ha. Hm.' The sergeant replaced the receiver and went back to Julian and the others. 'News has just come in that the kidnappers have contacted Mr Elbur Wright, and told him they've got his daughter Berta,' he said.

'Oh! And have they demanded that he shall tell them the secret figures he knows?' asked Julian.

The sergeant nodded. 'Yes. He's almost off his head with shock! He's promised to give them all they want. Very foolish!'

'Gosh – you'd better tell him it's *not* Berta they've got, but George,' said Dick. 'Then he'll sit tight!'

The sergeant frowned. 'Now, you leave this to *us*,' he said, ponderously. 'You'll only hinder us if you interfere or try meddling on your own. You just sit back and take things easy.'

'What! With George kidnapped and in danger?'

exploded Dick. 'What are *you* going to do to get her back?'

'Now, now!' said the sergeant, annoyed. 'She is in no danger – she's not the person they want. They will free her as soon as they realise that.'

'They won't,' said Dick. 'They'll get on to her father and make *him* give up a few secrets!'

'Well, that will give us a little more time to find these men,' said the irritating sergeant, and he stood up, big and burly in his navy blue uniform. 'Let me know *at once* if you have any other news, and please do not try to meddle. I assure you that we know the right things to do.'

He went out with the constable. Julian groaned. 'He doesn't see that this is *urgent*. It's so complicated too – the wrong girl kidnapped, the wrong father informed, the right one not at all inclined to give up powerful secrets – and poor old George not knowing what is happening!'

'Well, thank goodness we got *Berta* out of the way,' said Dick. 'Anne, you look funny – are you all right?'

'Yes. I think I'm just shocked – and oh dear, I feel awfully *empty*!' said Anne, pressing her tummy.

'Gosh – we forgot all about breakfast!' said Dick, staring at the clock. 'And it's almost ten o'clock now! What *have* we been doing all this time? Come on, Anne – get us some food, there's a dear. We shall all feel better then.'

'I'm so sorry for poor old Timmy and little Sally,' said Anne, going into the kitchen. 'Timmy, darling, don't look at me like that! I don't know *where* your beloved George is, or I'd take you to her straight away! And Sally, you will have to put up with me for a little while, because although I do know where Berta is, I can't possibly take you there!'

They were soon sitting down to a plain breakfast of

boiled eggs, toast and butter. It seemed strange only to
be three. Dick tried to make conversation, but the
other two were very quiet. Timmy sat under the table
with his head on Anne's foot, and Sally stood beside
her, paws on her knee. Anne comforted both the
mournful dogs as best she could!

After breakfast Anne went to wash up and make the
beds, and the boys went outside to have another look
at the place where George's dressing-gown girdle had
been found. Sally and Timmy came with them.

Timmy sniffed around a good bit, and then, nose to
ground went down the garden path to the front gate,
and then pushed it open and went through it. Nose to
ground he went down the lane and turned off into a
little path.

'Dick – he's following some kind of trail,' said
Julian. 'I'm certain it's George's. Even if somebody
carried her away, Timmy is clever enough to know
George might be with him – he might just get a whiff
of her.'

'Come on – let's follow Timmy,' said Dick, and the
boys and Sally went along the little path, hot on
Timmy's track. Timmy began to run, and Dick called
to him.

'Not so fast, old boy! We're coming too.'

But Timmy did not slow down. Whatever it was he
smelt, the scent was quite strong. The boys ran after
him, beginning to feel excited.

But soon Timmy came to a full stop, in a little
clearing in the wood. Dick and Julian panted up to
where he was nosing round. He looked up at them
forlornly. Evidently the scent came to an end there.

'Car-tracks!' said Dick, pointing down to where the
dampish grass under a great oak tree had been rutted
with big tyre-marks. 'See? The men brought a car here
and hid it, then crept through the woods to Kirrin

Cottage, and waited for a chance to get Berta. They got George instead – but they wouldn't have got *anyone* if only George hadn't been ass enough to take Sally to the kennel! The house was well and truly locked and bolted!'

Julian was looking at the wheel-tracks. 'These tracks were made by very big tyres,' he said. 'It was a car – and I rather think these are *American* tyre-marks. I can check that when I get back – I'll go and ask Jim at the local garage – he'll know. I'll just sketch one quickly.'

He took out a notebook and pencil and began to sketch. Dick bent down and looked more carefully at the tracks. 'There is quite a lot of criss-crossing of tracks,' he said. 'I think the men came here and waited. Then, when they got George, they must have pushed her into the car, and turned it to go back the way they came – see, the tracks lead down that wide path over there. They made a mess of the turning, though – bumped into this tree, look – there's a mark right across it.'

'Where?' said Julian at once. 'Yes – a bright blue mark – the car was that colour – or the wings were, at any rate. Well, that's something we've learnt! A big blue car, probably American. Surely the police could trace that?'

'Timmy's still nosing round, the picture of misery,' said Dick. 'Poor old Tim. I expect he knows George was pushed into a car just there. Hallo – he's scraping at something!'

They ran to see what it was. Timmy was trying to get at some small object embedded in a car-rut. Evidently, in turning, the car had run over whatever it was.

Dick saw something broken in half – something green. He picked up the halves. 'A comb! Did George have a little green comb like this?'

'Yes. She did,' said Julian. 'She must have thrown it down when she got near to the car – to show us she was taken here – hoping we would find it. And look, what's that?'

It was a handkerchief hanging on a gorse bush. Julian ran to it. It had the initial G on it in blue.

'Yes, it's George's,' he said. 'She's got six of these, all with different-coloured initials. She must have thrown this out too. Quick, Dick, look for anything else she might have thrown out of the car, while they were trying to turn it. They would probably put her in the back, and she would just have had a chance to throw out anything she had in her dressing-gown pocket, to let us know she was here if we came along this way.'

They searched for a long time. Timmy found one more thing, again embedded in a car-rut – a boiled sweet wrapped in cellophane paper.

'Look!' said Dick, picking it up. 'One of the sweets we all had the other night! George must have had one in her dressing-gown pocket! If only she had had a pencil and bit of paper – she might have had time to write a note too!'

'That's an idea!' said Julian. 'We'll hunt even more carefully!'

But although they searched every bit of ground and every bush, there was no note to be found. It was too much to hope for!

'Let's just follow the car-tracks and make sure they reached the road,' said Julian. So they followed them down the wide woodland path.

At the side a little way along, a piece of paper blew in the wind, hopping an inch or two each time the breeze flapped it. Dick picked it up – and then looked at Julian excitedly.

'She *did* have time to write a note! This is her writing. But there's only one word, look – whatever does it mean?'

Julian and Dick frowned over the piece of paper. Yes, it was George's writing – the G was exactly like the way she always wrote the big G at the beginning of her signature.

'Gringo,' read Julian. 'Just that one word. Gringo! What *does* it mean? It's something she heard them say, I suppose – and she just had time to write it and throw out the paper. Gringo! Timmy, what does *Gringo* mean?'

16 *Jo!*

Dick and Julian went back to Kirrin Cottage with the two disconsolate dogs. They showed Anne the things they had found, and she too puzzled over the word Gringo.

'We'll have to tell the police what you have discovered,' she said. 'They might trace the car, and they might know who or what Gringo is.'

'I'll telephone them now,' said Julian. 'Dick, you go down to the garage with this sketch of the tyre-mark, and see if it's an American design.'

The police were interested but not helpful. The sergeant said he would send his constable up to examine the place where the car had stood in the clearing, and gave it as his opinion that the bit of paper wasn't much use, as the boys had found it some way from the turning place of the car.

'Your cousin wouldn't be able to throw it out of the window once the car was going,' he said. 'There would be sure to be someone in the back with her. The only reason she could throw things out at the clearing would be because the second fellow – and there would certainly be two – would be guiding the other man in the turning of the car.'

'The wind might have blown the note along the path,' said Julian. 'Anyway, I've given you the information.'

It was a very miserable day, although the sun shone down warmly, and the sea was blue and most inviting.

But nobody wanted to bathe, nobody really wanted to do anything but talk and talk about George and what had happened, and where she could be at that moment!

Joanna came back in time to get their lunch, and was pleased to find that Anne had done the potatoes and prepared a salad, and that Dick had managed to pick some raspberries. They were very glad to see Joanna. She was someone sensible and comforting and matter-of-fact.

'Well, Jane is now safely in my cousin's cottage,' she said. 'She was very miserable but I told her she must smile and play about, else the neighbours would wonder about her. I put her into some of Jo's clothes – they fitted her all right. Hers are too expensive-looking, and would make people talk!'

They told Joanna what they had discovered in the clearing that morning. She took the note and looked at it. 'Gringo!' she said. 'That's a funny word – sounds like a traveller word to me. It's a pity Jo isn't here – she might tell us what it means!'

'Did you see Jo?' asked Dick.

'No. She was out shopping,' said Joanna, lifting the lid to look at the potatoes. 'I only hope she gets on with Jane all right. Really, it's getting very difficult to remember that child's change of names!'

The only fresh news that day was a worried telephone call from Aunt Fanny. She was shocked and amazed at the news she had heard. 'Your uncle has collapsed!' she said. 'He has been working very hard, you know, and now this news of George has been quite the last straw. He's very ill. I can't leave him at the moment – but anyway we couldn't *do* anything! Only the police can help now. To think those horrible men took George by mistake!'

'Don't worry too much, Aunt Fanny,' said Julian. 'We've hidden Berta away safely, and I expect the men will free George as soon as she tells them she's the wrong girl.'

'If she *does* tell them!' said Dick, under his breah. 'She might not, for Berta's sake, for a few days at any rate!'

Everyone went miserable to bed that night. Anne took Timmy and Sally with her, for both were so forlorn that she couldn't bear to do anything else. Timmy wouldn't eat anything at all, and Anne was worried about him.

Julian could not go to sleep. He tossed and turned, thinking about George. Hot-tempered, courageous, impatient, independent George! He worried and worried about her, wishing he could *do* something!

A small stone suddenly rattled against his window! He sat up, alert at once. Then something fell right into the room, and rolled over the floor. Julian was at the window in a trice. Who was throwing pebbles at his window?

He leaned out. A voice came up to him at once. 'Is it you, Dick?'

'Jo! What *are* you doing here?' said Julian, startled. 'It's Julian speaking. Dick's asleep. I'll wake him, and let you in.'

But he did not need to go down and let Jo in. She was up a tree outside the window and across some ivy and on his window-sill before he had even shaken Dick awake!

She slid into the room. Julian switched on his light. There was Jo, sitting at the end of Dick's bed, the familiar cheeky grin on her face! She was very brown, but still showed her freckles, and her hair was as short and curly as ever.

'I *had* to come,' she said. 'When I got home from shopping, there was this girl Jane. She told me all about how George had been captured in mistake for her – and when I said to her, "You go straight away and say you're safe and sound, and it's all a mistake, and George has got to be set free!" she wouldn't! She just wouldn't! All she did was to sit and cry. Little coward!'

'No, no, Jo,' said Dick, and tried to explain everything to the indignant girl. But he could not convince her.

'If I was that girl Jane I wouldn't let someone stay kidnapped because of *me*,' she said. 'I don't like her, she's silly. And I'm supposed to keep an eye on her! Phoo! Not me! I'd *like* her to be kidnapped, the way she's behaving about George.'

Julian looked at Jo. She was very, very loyal to the Five, and proud of being their friend. She had been in two adventures with them now, a crafty little traveller girl, but a very loyal friend. Her father was in prison, and she was living with a cousin of Joanna's, and, for the first time in her life, going to school to learn lessons!

'Listen, Jo – we've found out a few more things since Berta – I mean Lesley – no, I don't, I mean Jane . . .'

'What *do* you mean?' said Jo, puzzled.

'I mean Jane,' said Julian. 'We've found out something else since Joanna parked Jane with her cousin this morning.'

'Go on, tell me,' said Jo. 'Have you found out where George is? I'll go and break in and get her out, if you have!'

'Oh Jo – it's no use just being fierce,' said Dick. 'Things are not so easy as all that!'

'George threw out a bit of paper with this written on it,' said Julian, and he put it before Jo. 'See? Just that one word – "Gringo". Does it mean anything to you?'

'Gringo?' said Jo. 'That rings a bell! Let's see now – *Gringo*!'

She frowned as she thought hard. Then she nodded. 'Oh yes, I remember now. A fair came to the town a few weeks back – the big town not far from our village. It was called Gringo's Great Fair.'

'Where did it go?' asked Dick, eagerly.

'It was going to Fallenwick, then to Granton,' said Jo. 'I made friends with the boy whose father owned the roundabout, and gosh, I had about a hundred free rides.'

'You *would*!' said both boys together, and Jo grinned.

'Do you suppose this Gringo, who runs the Fair, could be anything to do with the name Gringo that George wrote on this paper?' said Julian.

'*I* dunno!' said Jo. 'But if you like I can go and find the fair and get hold of Spiky – that's the roundabout boy – and see if I can find out anything. I know Spiky said Gringo was a real horror to work for, and thought himself as good as a lord!'

'Had he a car – a big car?' asked Dick, suddenly.

'I dunno that either,' said Jo. 'I can find out. Here – I'll go *now*! You lend me a bike and I'll bike to Granton!'

'Certainly not,' said Julian, startled at the idea of Jo biking the twelve miles to Granton in the middle of the night.

'All right,' said Jo, rather sulkily. 'I just thought you'd like me to help. It might be that this Gringo has got George somewhere. He was the kind of fellow who was a go-between, if you know what I mean.'

'How?' asked Dick.

'Well, Spiky said that if anyone wanted something dirty done, this Gringo just held out his hand, and if a wad of notes was put into it, he'd do it, and nothing said!' said Jo.

'I see,' said Julian. 'Hm – it sounds as if kidnapping would be right up his street, then.'

Jo laughed scornfully. 'That would be nothing to him – chicken-feed. Come on, Julian – let me have a lend of your bike.'

'NO,' said Julian. 'Thanks very, very much, but I'm not letting anyone ride to a fair in the middle of the night to find out if a fellow called Gringo has anything to do with George. I can't believe he has, either – it's too far-fetched.'

'All right. But you *asked* me if the name meant anything to me,' said Jo, sounding offended. 'Anyway, it's a common enough nickname in the circus world and the fair world too. There's probably a thousand Gringos about!'

'It's time you went back home,' said Julian, looking at his watch. 'And be decent to Berta – I mean Jane – *please*, Jo. You can come over tomorrow to see if there's any more news. How did you get here tonight, by the way?'

'Walked,' said Jo. 'Well – ran, I mean. Not by the roads, though – they take too long. I go like the birds do – as straight as I can, and it's *much* shorter!'

Dick had a sudden picture of the valiant little Jo speeding through woods and fields, over hills and through valleys, as straight as a crow flying homewards. How did she find her way like that? He knew *he* would never be able to!

Jo slipped out over the window-sill, and down the tree, as easily as a cat. 'Bye!' she said. 'See you soon.'

'Give our love to Jane,' whispered Dick.

'Shan't!' said Jo, much too loudly, and disappeared.

Julian switched out the light. 'Whew!' he said, 'I always feel as if I've been blown about by a strong, fresh wind when I see Jo. What a girl! Fancy wanting to ride all the way to Granton tonight, after running all the way here from Berta's!'

'Yes. I'm jolly glad you wouldn't let her take your bike,' said Dick. 'It's a good thing she wouldn't dare to disobey you!'

He got into bed – and just at that very moment the two boys heard a loud ringing noise. Dick sat up straight away.

'Well I'm blowed!' he said. 'The little wretch!'

'What's up?' said Julian, and then he too realised what the ringing was – a bicycle bell. Yes, a bell rung loudly and defiantly by someone cycling swiftly along the sea-road towards Granton!

'It's *Jo*!' said Dick. 'And she's taken *my* bike! I know its bell. Gosh, won't I rub her face in the mud when I get hold of her!'

Julian gave a loud guffaw. 'She's a monkey, a gallant, plucky, loyal, aggravating *monkey*. What a cheek she's got! She didn't dare to take *my* bike when I'd said no – so she took yours. Well – we can't do a thing about it now. What that roundabout boy is going to think when he's woken in the middle of the night by Jo, I cannot imagine.'

'He's probably used to her,' said Dick. 'Well, let's go to sleep. I wonder if George is asleep or awake? I hate to think of her a prisoner somewhere.'

'I bet Timmy hates it more than we do,' said Dick, hearing a long-drawn whimper from the next room. 'Poor old Tim. He can't go to sleep either!'

Dick and Julian managed to go to sleep at last, both thinking of a speedy little figure on a bicycle, racing through the night to ask questions of a roundabout boy called Spiky!

17 To Gringo's Fair

At half past seven next morning Joanna came running upstairs to Julian's bedroom, a piece of paper in her hand. She knocked on the door.

'Julian! A dirty little note was on the front door mat when I got down this morning. It's folded over with your name on the outside.'

Julian was out of bed in a trice. A note from the kidnappers perhaps? No – it couldn't be. They wouldn't write to *him*!

It was from Jo! She had scribbled it so badly that Julian could hardly read it.

'Julian, I saw Spiky, he's coming to the beach at eleven. I took Dick's bike to go home on. I will bring it back at eleven, don't be too cross. Jo.'

'Little scallywag,' said Dick. 'I hope she hasn't damaged my bike in any way.'

Jo hadn't. She had actually managed to find time to clean it before she left home, and arrived with it so bright and gleaming that Dick hadn't the heart to scold her!

She was early so she came to the house instead of the beach. She rode through the gate and up the front path and Timmy ran to greet her with a volley of delighted barks. He liked Jo – in fact he really loved the little girl. She certainly had a way with animals! Sally followed, dancing on her tiptoes as usual, ready to welcome as a friend anyone that Timmy liked.

Dick hailed Jo from the front door as she came up.

'Hallo, bicycle-stealer! My word, what's happened to my bike – have you spring-cleaned it?'

Jo grinned, looking at Dick warily. 'Yes. I'm sorry I took it, Dick.'

'You're not a bit sorry – but I'll forgive you,' said Dick, grinning too. 'So you got to the fair safely after all?'

'Oh yes – and I woke up Spiky – he wasn't half surprised,' said Jo. 'But his pa was sleeping in the same caravan as he was, so I couldn't say much. I just told him to be on Kirrin Beach at eleven. Then I rode back home. I ought to have left your bike on the way back, but I was a bit tired, so I rode home, instead of walking.'

'You can't have had much sleep last night,' said Julian, looking at the sunburnt girl with her untidy curly hair. 'Hallo – who's that?'

A short, plump boy was hurrying past the gate. He had a mop of black hair which stuck up into curious spikes of hair at the crown.

'Oh – that's Spiky!' said Jo. 'He's on time, isn't he? He's called Spiky because of his hair. You won't believe it, but he spends a fortune on hair-oil, trying to make those spiky bits go flat. But they won't.' She called loudly.

'Spiky! Hey, SPIKY!'

Spiky turned at once. He had a pleasant, rather lop-sided face, and eyes as black as currants. He stood staring at Jo and the boys. 'I'm just off to the beach,' he said.

'Right. We're coming too,' said Jo, and she and the boys went to join him. They met the ice-cream man on the way and Julian bought an ice-cream for each of them.

'Coo – thanks,' said Spiky, pleased. He was rather shy of Dick and Julian, and wondered very much why he had been asked to come.

They sat down on the beach. 'I wasn't half scared when you came tapping at the window last night,' he said to Jo, licking his ice-cream with a very pink tongue. 'What's it all about?'

'Well,' said Julian, cautiously, 'we're interested in somebody called Gringo.'

'Old Gringo?' said Spiky. 'A lot of people're interested in Gringo. Do you know what we say at the fair? We say Gringo ought to put up a notice. "All dirty work done here!" He's a bad lot, Gringo is – but he pays us well, even if he makes us work like slaves.'

'He owns the fair, doesn't he?' said Julian, and Spiky nodded. 'I expect he uses it as a cover for all his other, bigger jobs,' Julian said to Dick. He looked at the plump, black-eyed boy, wondering how far he could trust him. Jo saw the look and knew what it meant.

'He's all right,' she said, nodding towards Spiky. 'You can say what you like. He's an oyster, he is. Aren't you, Spiky?'

Spiky grinned his lop-sided grin. Julian decided to trust him, and speaking in a low voice that really thrilled Spiky, he told him about the kidnapping of George. Spiky's eyes nearly fell out of his head.

'Coo!' he said. 'I bet old Gringo's at the bottom of that. Last week he went off up to London – he told my pa he was on to a big job – an American job, he said it was.'

'Yes – it sounds as if it all fits,' said Julian. 'Spiky, this kidnapping happened the night before last. Did anything unusual occur in the fair camp, do you know? It must have happened in the middle of the night.'

Spiky considered. He shook his head. 'No – I don't think so. Gringo's big double-caravan is still there – so he can't have gone. He had it moved right away from the camp yesterday morning – said there was too much noise for his old ma, who lives in his posh caravan and looks after him. We was all glad it was moved – now he can't spy on us so easily!'

'I suppose you . . .' began Julian, and then stopped as Dick gave an exclamation.

'I've got an idea!' he said. 'Suppose that caravan was moved for *another* reason – suppose someone was making a row inside the van – someone shouting for help, say! Gringo would have to move it away from the rest of the camp in case that someone was heard.'

There was a pause, and then Spiky nodded. 'Yes. It could be,' he said. 'I've never known Gringo move his caravan away from the camp before. Shall I do a bit of snooping for you?'

'Yes,' said Julian, excited. 'My word – it *would* be a bit of luck if we could find George so quickly – and so near us too! A fair camp would be a fine place to hide her, of course. Thank goodness we found that bit of paper with "Gringo" written on it!'

'Let's all go to the fair this afternoon,' said Dick. 'Timmy too. He'd smell out George at once.'

'Hadn't we better tell the police first?' said Julian. At once Spiky and Jo got up in alarm. Spiky looked as if he were going to run away immediately!

'Don't you get the police, Julian!' said Jo urgently. 'You won't get anything more out of Spiky, if you do. Not a thing.'

'I'm going,' said Spiky, still looking terrified.

'No, you're not,' said Dick, and caught hold of him. 'We shan't go to the police. They might frighten off Gringo and make him smuggle George away at once. I've no doubt he has plans to do so at any minute. We shan't say a word, so sit down and be sensible.'

'You can believe him,' Jo told Spiky. 'He's straight, see?'

Spiky sat down, still looking wary. 'If you're coming to the fair, come at four,' he said. 'It's half-day closing today for the towns around, and the place will be packed. If you want to do any snooping, you won't be noticed in that crowd.'

'Right,' said Julian. 'We'll be there. Look out for us, Spiky, in case you've got any news.'

Spiky then left, and the boys couldn't help smiling at his back view – the spikes of hair at the top of his head were so very noticeable!

'You'd better stay to lunch with us, Jo,' said Dick, and the delighted girl beamed all over her face.

'Will Joanna's cousin mind you not being back to dinner?' asked Julian.

'No. I said I wouldn't be back all day,' said Jo. 'It's still school holidays, you see. Anyway, I can't stand that Jane – she moons about all the time – and she's got some of my clothes on, too.'

Jo sounded so indignant about Berta that the boys had to laugh. They all went back to Kirrin Cottage, and found Joanna and Anne hard at work in the house.

'Well, you monkey!' said Joanna to Jo. 'Up to tricks as usual, I hear. Throwing stones at people's windows in the middle of the night. You just try that, on *my* window and see what happens to you! Now, put on that apron, and help round a bit. How's Jane?'

Joanna was most excited to hear about the boys' latest ideas as to where George might be. Julian gave her a warning.

'But no ringing up the police behind our backs *this* time, Joanna,' he said. 'This is something best done by Dick and me.'

'Can't I come with Sally?' asked Anne.

'We can't *possibly* take Sally,' said Dick, 'in case Gringo's about and recognises her. So you'd better stay and look after her, and we'll take Timmy. He would be sure to smell where George is, if she's hidden anywhere in the camp. But I think she's probably in Gringo's own caravan.'

Timmy pricked up his ears every time he heard George's name mentioned. He was a very miserable dog indeed, and kept running to the front gate, hoping to see George coming along. Whenever they missed him, they knew where to find him – lying mournfully on George's empty bed – probably with an equally mournful Sally beside him!

The boys and Jo set off to the fair about half past three, on their bicycles. Jo rode Anne's this time, and Timmy ran valiantly beside them. Jo glanced at Dick's bicycle from time to time, proud of its brilliant look – how well she had cleaned it that morning!

They came to the fair. 'You can put your bikes up against Spiky's caravan,' said Jo. 'They'll be safe there. Will you pay, and then we'll get in straightaway? You needn't pay for me – I'm going through the gap in the hedge. I'm Spiky's friend, so it's all right.'

She gave Dick her bicycle and disappeared. Julian paid and went in at the gate. They saw Jo waving wildly to them from the side of the big field and wheeled the three bicycles over to her, Timmy followed closely at their heels.

'Hallo!' said Spiky, appearing suddenly. 'See you soon! I've got to go and tend to the roundabout. I've got a bit of news, but not much. That's Gringo's caravan over there, the double one, big van in front, little van behind.'

He nodded his head to where a most magnificent caravan stood, right away from the rest of the camp. There were people milling about all round the other vans, but there was nobody at all by Gringo's. Evidently no one dared to go too near.

'I vote we buy a ball at one of the stands, and then go

and play near Gringo's caravan,' said Dick, in a low voice. 'Then one of us will throw the ball too hard and it will go near the van – and we'll somehow manage to get a peep inside. Timmy can go sniffing round while we play. If George is there he'll bark the place down.'

'Jolly good idea!' said Julian. 'Come on, Jo! And keep your eyes open all the time in case you've got to warn us of danger.'

18   Spiky is very helpful

The two boys and Jo, with Timmy at their heels, wandered round the fair to find somewhere to buy a ball. There seemed to be none for sale, so they had a go at a Hoopla stall, and Julian managed to get a ring round a small red ball. Just the thing!

It was a big and noisy fair, and hundreds of people from the nearby towns had come on this shops' closing day to enjoy the fun. The roundabout played its loud, raucous music all the time, swings went to and fro, the dodgem cars banged and bumped one another as usual, and men went round shouting their wares.

'Balloons! Giant balloons! Fifty pence each!'

'Ice-cream! All flavours.'

'Tell your fortune, lady? I'll tell it true as can be!'

Jo was very much at home in the fair. She had been brought up in one, and knew all the tricks of the trade. Timmy was rather amazed at the noise, and kept close to the boys, his tail still down because he could not forget that George was missing.

'Now let's play our little game of ball,' said Julian. 'Come on, Tim – and if we get into any trouble, just growl and show your teeth, see?'

The three of them, with Timmy, went to the clear space of field that separated the magnificent caravan from the rest of the camp. A man at a nearby stall called to them.

'Hey! You'll get into trouble if you play there!' But

they took no notice and he shrugged his shoulders and began to shout his wares.

They threw the ball to one another, and then Julian flung it so wildly that it ran right up to the wheels of the front caravan of the pair. In a trice Dick and Jo were after it. Jo leapt up on a wheel and looked in at the big window, while Dick ran to the small van that was attached behind the big one.

A quick glance assured Jo that the big caravan was empty. The interior was furnished in a most luxurious way and looked like a very fine bed-sitting-room. She leapt down.

Dick peered into the window of the smaller van. At first he thought there was no one there – and then he saw a pair of very fierce, angry eyes looking at him – the eyes of a small, bent old woman with untidy hair. She looked rather like a witch, Dick thought. She was sitting sewing on a bunk, and, as he looked in, she shook her fist at him and called out something he couldn't hear.

He jumped down and joined the others. 'No one at all in the big van,' said Jo.

'Only a witch-like old woman in the other,' reported Dick, in deep disappointment. 'Unless George is pushed under a bunk or squashed into a cupboard, she's certainly not there!'

'Timmy doesn't seem interested in the caravans at all, does he?' said Julian. 'I'm sure if George really *was* in one of those caravans, he'd bark and try to get inside.'

'Yes – I think he would,' said Dick. 'Hallo, there's somebody coming out of the second van. It's the old lady! She's in a fine old temper!'

So she was! She came down the steps to the van, shouting and shaking her fist at them. 'Tim – go and find, go and find – in that van!' said Julian, suddenly, as the old woman came towards them.

The three of them stood their ground as the old woman came right up. They couldn't understand a word she said, partly because she had no teeth, and partly because she spoke a mixture of many languages. Anyway, it was quite obvious that she was ticking them off for daring to play near the two vans.

Timmy had understood what Julian had said, and had slipped inside the second van. He was there for half a minute, and then he barked. The boys jumped, and Dick made a move towards the van.

Then Timmy appeared, dragging something behind him with his teeth. He tried to bark at the same time, but he couldn't. He dragged the coat-like thing right down to the ground before the old woman was on him, screaming in a high voice, and hitting him. She pulled the garment away and went up the steps, kicking out at the surprised Timmy as he tried to pull it away. The door slammed.

'If that old woman hadn't been old, Timmy would have soon shown her he was top dog!' said Dick. 'Whatever was he pulling out of the van?'

'Come over here, out of sight of the van,' said Julian, urgently. 'Didn't you recognise it, Dick? It was *George's dressing-gown*!'

'My word!' said Dick, stopping in surprise. 'Yes, you're right – it was. Whew! What does that mean exactly? George certainly isn't in those vans, or Timmy would have found her.'

'I sent him in to see if he could *smell* that George had been hidden there,' said Julian. 'I thought he would bark excitedly if he smelt her scent anywhere – on the bunk, perhaps. I never guessed he'd find her *dressing-gown* and drag it out to show us!'

'Good old Timmy! Clever old Timmy!' said Dick, patting the dog, whose tail was now at half-mast instead of right down. He had at least found George's dressing-gown – but how surprising to find it in that caravan!

'Why on earth didn't they take the dressing-gown with them, when they took George off?' wondered Julian. 'There's no doubt that she has *been* in that caravan – she was taken straight there the night before last, I expect. Where is she now?'

'She must have been dressed differently,' said Dick. 'They must have had to dress her properly, when they took her somewhere else. After all, she was only in pyjamas and dressing-gown.'

Jo was listening to all this, puzzled and worried. She nudged Dick. 'Spiky's beckoning to us,' she said. They went over to the roundabout boy, whose father was now in charge of the noisy machine.

Spiky took them into his caravan, a small and rather dirty one, in which he lived with his father.

'I saw Gringo's old ma chasing you!' he said with his lop-sided grin. 'What was your dog dragging out of the van?'

They told him. He nodded. 'I've been asking round a bit, cautiously,' he said, 'just to see if anyone had heard anything from Gringo's caravan – and the fellow whose caravan is nearest told me he heard shouts and yells two nights ago. He reckoned it was someone in Gringo's van – but he's too scared of Gringo to go and interfere, of course.'

'That would be George yelling,' said Dick.

'Well, then Gringo's vans were moved the next day right away from the other vans,' said Spiky. 'And this afternoon, before the fair opened, Gringo got his car and towed the little van – the second one – out of the field, and set off with it. We all wondered why, but he told somebody it needed repairing.'

'Whew! And George was inside!' said Dick. 'What a

cunning way of moving her off to another hiding place.'

'When did the van come back?' asked Julian.

'Just before you came,' said Spiky. 'I don't know where it went. It was gone an hour, I should think.'

'An hour,' said Dick. 'Well, suppose it goes at an averge of 25 miles an hour – you can't go very fast if you are towing something – that would mean he had gone somewhere about 12 miles or so away, and come back the same distance – making about an hour's drive, allowing for a stop when they arrived at the place they had to leave her at.'

'Yes,' said Julian. 'But there are lots of places within the radius of 12 miles!'

'Where's Gringo's *car*?' said Dick suddenly.

'Over there, under that big tarpaulin,' said Spiky. 'It's a silver-grey one – American and very striking. He thinks the world of it, Gringo does.'

'I'm going to have a peep at it,' said Julian, and strode off. He came to the tarpaulin, which covered the car right to the ground. He lifted it and was just about to look under it when a man ran up, shouting.

'Here, you! Leave that alone! You'll be turned out of the fair if you mess about with things that don't concern you!'

But Timmy was with Julian, and he turned and growled so fiercely that the man stopped in a hurry. Julian had plenty of time to take a good look under the tarpaulin!

Yes – the car was silver-grey, a big American one – and the wings were bright blue! Julian took a quick look at the two left-hand ones and saw a deep scratch on one of them. Before he dropped the tarpaulin he had time to glance at the tyres. He was sure they had the same pattern as those shown in the wheel-tracks he had sketched! He had checked the sketch with Jim, at Kirrin Garage, who had told him they were an American design.

Yes – this was the car that had hidden in the clearing the night before last – the car that had turned with difficulty and made those deep ruts – the car that had taken George away, and this afternoon had towed away the caravan with her inside, to hide her somewhere else.

He dropped the tarpaulin and walked back to the others, excited, taking no notice of the rude things that the nearby man called out to him.

'It's the car, all right,' said Julian. 'Now – WHERE did it go this afternoon? If only we could find out!'

'It's such a very striking car that anyone would notice it – especially as it was towing a rather nice little caravan,' said Dick.

'Yes – but we can't go round the countryside asking everyone we meet if they've noticed a silver-grey car with blue wings,' said Julian.

'Let's go back home and get a map and see the lie of the country round about,' said Dick. 'Spiky, which way did the car turn when it went out of the field gate?'

'Towards the east,' said Spiky. 'On the road to Big Twillingham.'

'Well, that's something to know,' said Dick. 'Come on, let's get our bikes. Thanks a lot, Spiky. You've been a terrific help. We'll let you know what happens.'

'Call on me if ever you want more help,' said Spiky, proudly, and gave them a smart little salute, bobbing his head so that his spikes of hair shook comically.

The three of them rode off, with Timmy running beside them again. As soon as they got home they told Anne and Joanna all they had found out. Joanna was for ringing up the police at once again, but Julian stopped her.

'I think perhaps we can do this next bit of work better than they can,' he said. 'We're going to try and find out where the car went, Joanna. Now – where are the maps of the district?'

They found them and began to pore over them. Jo was quite lost when it came to map-reading. She could find her way anywhere, day or night – but not with a map!

'Now – here's the road to Big Twillingham and Little Twillingham,' he said. 'Let's list carefully all the roads the car could take from there. My word – it's a job!'

19   *An exciting plan*

After fifteen minutes they had six towns on their list, all of which could have been reached in about half-an-hour from Big Twillingham, which was two miles away from the fair.

'And *now* what do you propose to do, Ju?' asked Dick. 'Bike over to all the towns and ask if anyone has seen the car?'

'No. We can't possibly do that,' said Julian. 'I'm going down to the garage to see our friend Jim, and get *his* help! I'm going to ask him to ring up any friends he has in the garages in those towns, and ask if they've seen the car passing through.'

'Won't he think it's a bit funny?' asked Anne.

'Yes. But he won't mind how funny it is if we pay the telephone calls and give him some money for his trouble!' said Julian, folding up the map. 'And what's more he won't ask any questions either. He'll probably think it's some silly bet we've got on with one another.'

Jim was quite willing to ring up the garages for them. He knew boys working in main garages in four of the towns, and he knew the hall porter of a hotel in the fifth town. But he knew no one in the sixth.

'That doesn't matter!' he said. 'We'll ring up the garage in the High Street there, and just ask whoever comes to the phone.'

Jim rang up the garage in Hillingford, and had a rather cheeky conversation with his friend there. He put the receiver down. 'No go,' he said. 'He says no car like that came through Hillingford, or he'd have noticed it that time of day. I'll ring up Jake at Green's Garage in Lowington now.'

'That's no go, either,' he said, after a minute's telephone conversation. 'I'll try my hall porter now. He's a cousin of mine.'

The hall porter had some news. 'Yes!' Jim kept saying. 'Yes, that's the one! Yes, yes! You heard him say that, did you? Thanks a lot.'

'What is it?' asked Dick, eagerly, when Jim at last put down the receiver.

'Pat – that's the hall porter – says he was off duty this afternoon, and went to buy some cigarettes at a little shop in the main street of Graysfield, where his hotel is – and as he stood talking to the fellow in the shop an enormous car drew up at the kerb – silver-grey, with blue wings – an American car, left-hand drive and all.'

'Yes – what next?' said Julian, eagerly.

'Well, the driver got out to get some cigarettes at the shop. He had dark glasses on, and a big gold ring on his finger – Pat noticed that . . .'

'That must be the man who asked about us at the tea-shop in Kirrin!' said Julian, remembering. 'Go on, Jim – this is wonderful!'

'Well, Pat's interested in big cars, so he went out and had a good look at it,' said Jim. 'He said the car had its blinds drawn down at the back, so he couldn't see inside. The fellow with the dark glasses came out and got into the driver's seat again. He called out to whoever was behind and said "Which way now?"'

'Yes, yes – did he hear the answer?' said Julian.

'Somebody called back and said, "Not far now. Into Twining, turn to the left, and it's the house on the hill."'

'*Well!* Of all the luck!' said Dick. 'Would that be where G . . .' He stopped at a sharp nudge from Julian, and remembered that he mustn't give too much away to the helpful Jim.

Julian passed over a pound to the pleased garage boy, who pocketed it at once, grinning. 'Now, you just come along to me if you want to know about any more cars,' he said. 'I'll phone all over the place for you! Thanks a lot!'

They sped back to Kirrin Cottage, too excited even to talk. They flung their bicycles against the wall and ran in to tell Anne and Joanna. Timmy and Sally sensed their excitement and danced round, barking loudly.

'We know where George is!' cried Dick. 'We know, we know!'

Joanna and Anne listened eagerly. 'Well, Julian,' said Joanna, in admiration, 'it was really smart of you to make Jim phone up like that. The police couldn't have done better. What are you going to do now? Ring up that sergeant?'

'No,' said Julian. 'I'm so afraid that if the police get moving on this now, they'll alarm Gringo and he'll spirit George away somewhere else. Dick and I will go to this place tonight, and see if we can't get hold of George and bring her back! After all – it's only an ordinary house, I imagine – and as Gringo doesn't suspect that anyone knows where George is, he won't be on the look-out!'

'Good!' said Dick. 'Good, good, good!'

'I'm coming too,' said Jo.

'You are not,' said Julian, at once. 'That's flat – you are NOT COMING, Jo. But I shall take Timmy, of course.'

Jo said no more, but looked so sulky that Anne laughed. 'Cheer up, Jo. You can keep me and Sally company. Oh Julian – wouldn't it be *wonderful* to find George and rescue her!'

There was more map-reading as the boys decided which was the best way to bicycle over to Graysfield. 'Look out the best torches we've got, Anne, will you?' said Dick. 'and let me see – how can we bring George back once we've got her? On my bike-step, I think, though I know it's not allowed. But this is very urgent. We can't very well take a third bike with us. Gosh, isn't this exciting!'

'We really ought to ring up the police,' said Joanna, who kept saying this at intervals.

'Joanna, you sound like a parrot!' said Julian. 'If we're not back by morning you can ring up all the police in the country if you want to!'

'There's been another phone call from your aunt today, Julian – I nearly forgot to tell you,' said Joanna. 'Your uncle is better and they are coming home as soon as possible.'

'Not this evening, I hope,' said Julian, in alarm. 'Did they tell you anything about Mr Elbur Wright – Berta's father?'

'Oh, he's hanging on to his secrets quite happily now that he knows it isn't Berta who is kidnapped,' said Joanna. 'I don't know if the kidnappers even know they've got the wrong girl yet. It's all very hush-hush. Even your uncle and aunt are having to obey the police. Your poor aunt is so terribly upset about George.'

'Yes. She must be frightfully worried,' said Julian, soberly. 'We've had so much excitement today that I've almost forgotten to worry. And anyway when you're able to *do* something, things don't seem so bad.'

'Be careful you don't go and do too much and land yourself in trouble,' said Joanna, darkly.

'I'll be careful!' said Julian, winking at Dick. 'I say – isn't it nearly supper-time? I feel awfully hungry.'

'Well, we haven't had any tea. No wonder we're hungry.'

'Would you like bacon and eggs for a treat?' said Joanna, and there was a chorus of approval at once. Timmy and Sally wagged their tails as if Joanna's question applied to them too!

'We'll set off as soon as it's dark,' said Julian. 'Jo, you'd better go home after supper. They'll be worrying about you.'

'All right,' said Jo, pleased to have been asked to supper, but still sulky at being forbidden to go with Julian and Dick that night.

Jo disappeared after supper, with many messages to Berta from Dick, Julian, Anne and Sally.

'And I bet she doesn't give a single one of them!' said Dick. 'Now, let's have a game before we set off, Julian. Just to take our minds off the excitement. I'm getting all worked up!'

Joanna went up to bed at ten because she was tired. Anne stayed up to see the boys off. 'You *will* be careful,' she kept saying. 'You *will* be careful, won't you? Oh dear, I think it's almost worse to stay behind and wonder what's happening to you, than to go with you and find out!'

At last the time came for the boys to go. It was a quarter to twelve and, except for a small moon, was a dark night, with great clouds looming up, often hiding the moon.

'Come on, Timmy,' said Dick. 'We're going to find George.'

'Woof!' said Timmy, delighted. Sally wuffed too, and was most disappointed at being left behind. The boys wheeled their bicycles to the front gate.

'So long, Anne!' said Dick. 'Go to bed – and hope to

see George when you wake up!'

They set off on their bicycles, with Timmy loping along beside them. They soon arrived at the field where the fair was, and went swinging away to the east, following the road the silver-grey car had gone that afternoon.

They knew the way by heart, for they had studied the map so well. As they passed the signposts they felt their excitement beginning to mount. 'Graysfield next,' said Dick at last. 'Soon be there, Timmy! You're not getting tired, are you?'

They came into Graysfield silently. The town was asleep, and not a single light showed in any window. A policemen suddenly loomed up out of the shadows, but when he saw two boys cycling, he did not stop them.

'Now – into Twining village, turn to the left – and look for the house on the hill!' said Dick.

They rode through the tiny, silent village of Twining, and took the lane to the left. It led up a steep, narrow lane. The boys had to get off and walk because the hill was too much for them.

'There's the house!' said Julian, suddenly whispering. 'Look – through those trees. My word, it looks a dark and lonely one!'

They came to some enormous iron gates, but when they tried to open them, they found them locked. A great wall ran completely round the grounds. They followed it a little way, leaving their bicycles against a tree by the gate, but it was soon certain that nobody could climb a wall like that!

'Blow!' said Julian. 'Blow!'

'What about the gates?' whispered Dick. Then he glanced round him nervously, hearing a twig crack. 'Did your hear that? There's nobody following us, is there?'

'No! Don't get the jitters, for goodness sake!' said Julian. 'What was it you were saying?'

'I said "What about the gates?"' said Dick. 'I don't see why we can't climb over them, do you? Nobody would do that in the daytime, they'd be seen – but I can't see why we can't do it *now* – they didn't look too difficult – just ordinary wrought-iron ones.'

'Yes! Of course!' said Julian. 'That's a brain wave. Come on!'

20 A thrilling time

The two boys went back to the gates. Dick turned round and looked behind him two or three times. 'I do hope nobody *is* shadowing us!' he said. 'I keep on feeling somebody's watching us all the time.'

'Oh, stuff!' said Julian, impatiently. 'Look – here are the gates. Give me a leg-up and I'll be over in a jiffy.'

Dick gave him a shove, and Julian climbed over the gates without much difficulty. They were bolted, not locked. He slid the great bolts carefully, and opened one gate a little for Dick and Timmy. 'Timmy can't be left behind!' he said. 'And he certainly couldn't climb this gate!'

They kept to the shadowed side of the drive as they walked up towards the house. The small moon came out from behind a cloud as they came near. It was an old house, with high chimneys, an ugly house with narrow windows that seemed like watching eyes.

Dick glanced behind him suddenly and Julian saw him. 'Got the jitters again?' he said, impatiently. 'Dick, don't be an ass. You know perfectly well that if anyone was shadowing us, Timmy would hear them and go for them at once.'

'Yes, I know,' said Dick. 'I'm an idiot – but I've just got that feeling tonight – the feeling that someone else *is* there!'

They came right up to the house. 'How shall we get in?' whispered Julian. 'The doors are all sure to be locked. We'll have to try the windows.'

They tiptoed silently round the big house. As Julian had said, the doors were all locked. The windows were all fastened too – well and truly fastened. Not one was open or could be opened.

'If this is a house belonging to Gringo he must be able to hide plenty of things in absolute safety – bolted gates, high walls, locked doors, fastened windows!' said Dick. 'No burglar could possibly get in.'

'And neither can we,' said Julian, desperately. 'We've been all round the house three times now! There's no door, no window we can get in. No balcony to climb up to – no ivy to hang on to – nothing!'

'Let's go round once more,' said Dick. 'We *might* have missed something.'

So once more they went round – and discovered something curious when they got to the kitchen quarters. The moon came out, and showed them a round black hole in the ground! Whatever could it be?

They tiptoed to it just as the moon went in again. They shone their torches on it briefly.

'It's a coal-hole!' said Dick, astonished. '*Why* didn't we see it before? Look, there's the lid just beside it. It's been left open. I suppose the moon was in last time we came by this part of the house. I can't think how we didn't notice it.'

Julian was uneasy. 'I didn't see it before, certainly. It's strange. Could it be a trap, do you think?'

'I don't see how it could be,' said Dick. 'Come on – let's get down. At least it's a way in.' He shone his torch into the hole. 'Yes, look – there's a whole lot of coke down there – we can easily jump on to it. Tim, you go first and spy out the land.'

Timmy jumped down at once, the coke slithering away from beneath his four paws. 'He's down all right,' said Julian. 'I'll go next. Then you.'

Down they jumped, and the coke slithered away again, making what seemed to be a very loud noise in the silent night. Julian shone his torch around.

They were standing on a very large heap of coke in the middle of a big cellar. At the end was a door.

'Hope it's not locked,' said Dick, in a whisper. 'Now, Tim, keep to heel, for goodness sake, and don't make a sound!'

They went to the door, treading on gritty bits of coke. Julian turned the dirty handle – and the door opened inwards! 'It's not locked!' said Julian, thankfully.

They crept through it, Timmy treading on their heels, and found themselves in another cellar, set with stone shelves on which were piled tins and boxes and crates. 'Enough food here to stand a siege!' whispered Dick. 'Where are the cellar steps? We've got to get out.'

'Over there,' said Julian. Then he stopped and put out his torch. He had heard something.

'Did you hear that?' he whispered. 'It sounded like somebody treading on the coke in the coal-cellar! Gosh, I hope nobody *is* shadowing us. We'll soon be prisoners if so.'

They listened but heard nothing further. Up the stone steps they went and undid the door at the top. A big kitchen lay beyond, lit by the dim moon. A shadow rose suddenly in front of them and Timmy growled. Dick's heart almost stopped beating. What in the world was that, crawling silently over the floor and disappearing in the shadows? He clutched at Julian and made him jump.

'Don't do that, ass! That was only the kitchen cat you saw,' whispered Julian. 'Gosh, you made me jump. Wasn't it a good thing that Timmy didn't go for the cat? There would have been an awful yowling!'

'Where do you suppose George will be?' asked Dick. 'Somewhere at the top of the house?'

'I've no idea. We'll just have to look into every room,' said Julian. So they looked into every room on the ground floor, but they were empty. They were huge rooms, ugly and over-furnished.

'Come on – up the stairs!' said Dick, and up they went. They came to an enormous landing, hung with tapestry curtains at the windows. Timmy suddenly gave a small growl and in a trice both boys had hidden themselves in the folds of the long window-curtains. Timmy went with them, feeling surprised. Dick peeped out after a minute.

'I think it was that cat again,' he whispered. 'Look, there it is, up on that chest. It's following us, wondering what on earth we're doing, I expect!'

'Blow it!' said Julian. '*I'm* getting the jitters now, being watched by a shadowy cat. I suppose it *is* real?'

'Timmy thinks so!' said Dick. 'Come on – there are any amount of bedroom doors on this landing.'

They tiptoed into the ones whose doors were open, but no one was sleeping in the beds there. They came to a closed door and listened. Someone was snoring inside!

'That's not George,' said Dick. 'Anyway, she'd be locked in, and the key is in this door.'

They went to the next door, which was also shut. They listened and could hear someone breathing heavily.

'Not George,' said Dick, and they went on up to the next flight of stairs. There were four more rooms there, two of them not even furnished. The doors of the other two were ajar, and it was clear that people were sleeping in them, because once more there was loud breathing to be heard.

'There don't seem to be any more rooms,' said

Dick, in dismay, as they flashed their torches carefully round the top landing. 'Blow! Where's George then?'

'Look – there's a little wooden door there,' said Julian, in Dick's ear. 'A door leading into the cistern room, I should think.'

'She wouldn't be there,' said Dick. 'But wait – look, there's a strong bolt on the door! And cistern rooms don't have bolts on their doors, or even locks. This one hasn't a lock, but it *has* a bolt.'

'Sh! Not so loud!' said Julian. 'Yes, that's funny, I must say. How can we get the door open without waking the people in those other two rooms?'

'We'll shut their doors very quietly, and we'll lock them!' said Dick, excited. 'I'll go and do it.'

He drew the doors gently to, and then locked first one and then the other, having taken the keys from the other side of the doors to do so. Except that one made a slight click as he locked it, there was no noise. Nobody stirred in the two rooms, and the boys breathed freely again.

They went to the little wooden door opposite. They pulled gently at the bolt, afraid that it might squeak. But it didn't. It was obviously quite new, and ran easily. The door opened outwards with a small creak. There was pitch darkness inside, and the sound of trickling water from the cistern.

Dick flashed his torch on and off quickly. In that second he saw something that made his heart jump!

There was a small mattress on the floor of the little cistern room, and someone was lying on it, rolled so completely in blankets that even the head was covered! Julian had seen it too, and he put his arm on Dick's, afraid that it might not be George, afraid that it might be someone who would give the alarm, perhaps another prisoner.

But Timmy knew who it was! Timmy ran straight

in with a small, loving whimper and flung himself on the sleeping figure!

Dick shut the cistern room door at once, afraid of the noise being heard. Timmy might bark with joy in a moment, or George might shout!

The figure gave a grunt and sat up. The blanket fell away from the head – and there was George's curly nob, and her startled face.

'Sh!' said Dick, raising his finger warningly. 'SH!' Timmy was licking George from head to foot, wild with delight, but extraordinarily silent – clever old Timmy knew that this was one of the times when joy must be dumb!

'Oh!' said George, hugging Timmy anywhere she could. 'Oh, Timmy! I missed you so! Darling, darling, Tim! Oh Timmy!'

Dick stood by the closed door, listening to find out if anyone was stirring in the other rooms. He heard nothing at all. Julian went to George.

'Are you all right, George?' he asked. 'Have you been treated well?'

'Not very,' said George. 'But then I didn't behave very well! I did quite a lot of kicking and biting – so they locked me in here!'

'Poor old George!' said Julian. 'Well, we'll hear everything when we've got out of here. So far, we've been jolly lucky. Can you come now?'

'Yes,' said George and got off the mattress. She was dressed in an odd selection of clothes, and looked rather peculiar. 'That awful old woman – Gringo's mother – found these for me when I was taken to the caravan,' she said. 'Gosh, I've got a lot to tell you!'

'Sh!' said Dick, at the door. 'Not a sound, now! I'm going to open the door!'

He opened it slowly. All was quiet. 'Now we'll go down the stairs,' he said. 'Not a sound!'

They went down the first flight of stairs and on to the enormous landing. Then, just as Dick put his foot on to the next stair down, he trod on something soft that yowled, spat and scratched. It was that cat!

Dick fell halfway down the stairs, and Timmy could not stop himself from chasing the cat up the landing and up the top stairs to the cistern room. Nor could he stop himself from barking!

Shouts came from two of the nearby bedrooms and two men appeared in pyjamas. One switched on the landing light, and then both of them tore down the stairs after the three children. Dick picked himself up, but he had ricked his ankle and could not even walk!

'Run, George – I'll see to Dick!' yelled Julian. But George stopped too – and in a trice the two men were on to them, catching hold of Dick and Julian, and jerking them into a nearby room.

'Tim! TIM!' shouted George. 'Help, Timmy!'

But before Timmy could come pelting down the stairs from the attic George was shoved into the room too, and the door locked.

'Look out for the dog!' shouted one of the men. 'He's dangerous!'

Timmy certainly was! He came tearing towards the men, snarling, his eyes blazing, showing all his teeth.

The men darted into the room next to the one into which they had locked the children, and banged the door. Timmy flung himself against it in rage, snarling and growling in a most terrifying manner. If only he could get at those men! If only he could!

21   Most unexpected!

Soon there was real pandemonium in the old house! The sleepers in the rooms on the top landing awoke suddenly and found their doors locked, and began to bang on them and shout. The three children in the locked room on the ground floor shouted and banged too – and Timmy nearly went mad!

Only the men in the room next to the children were silent. They were terrified at Timmy's growling and snarling. They would have liked to lock themselves in, but the key was on the other side of the door – and they certainly didn't dare to open it to get the key!

Soon the children quietened down. Dick sat on a chair, exhausted. 'That cat! That wretched, prowling, sly old cat! Gosh, I stepped on it and it scratched me to the bone – to say nothing of pitching me headlong down the stairs and making me wrench my ankle!'

'We so *nearly* managed to escape!' groaned Julian.

'I can't *think* what will happen now!' said George. 'Timmy's out there and can't get in to us, and we can't possibly get out to him because the door's locked – and those men won't dare to set a foot outside *their* door while Tim's there!'

'And we've locked the people into their rooms upstairs!' said Julian. 'Well, it's certain that nobody can get out of their rooms to help anyone else – so it looks as if we'll all be here till Doomsday!'

It certainly did seem a very poor look-out. The only people who were not behind locked doors were the two men, whoever they were – and they simply dared not put a foot outside their room. Timmy roamed about, occasionally whimpering and scratching outside the children's door, but more often growling outside the next door, sometimes flinging his heavy body against it as if he would break it down.

'I bet the men are shaking with fright,' said Dick. 'They won't even dare to try and get out of a window in case they meet Timmy outside somewhere!'

'Serve them right,' said George. 'Gosh, I'm glad you came! Wasn't I an absolute ass to take Sally down to the kennel that night?'

'You were,' said Julian, 'I agree wholeheartedly. The men were waiting for a chance to get Berta, of course, and they saw you, complete with Berta's dog, and thought you were the girl they wanted!'

'Yes. They flung something all over my head so that I couldn't make a sound,' said George. 'I fought like anything, and my dressing-gown girdle must have slipped off – did you find it?'

'Yes,' said Dick. 'We were jolly glad to find a few other things too – the comb – the hanky – the sweet – and of course the note!'

'They carried me quite a way to somewhere in the wood,' said George. 'Then they plonked me down in the back of the car. But they had to turn it and it was difficult – and I had the bright thought of throwing out all the things in my dressing-gown pocket just in *case* you came along and saw them.'

'What about that note – with the word Gringo on?' asked Julian. 'That was a terrific help. We wouldn't be here tonight if it hadn't been for that.'

'Well, I heard one of the men call the other Gringo,' said George. 'And it was such an unusual name I thought I'd scribble it on a bit of paper and throw that out too – it was just on chance I did it.'

'A jolly good chance!' said Dick. 'Good thing you had a notebook and pencil with you!'

'I hadn't,' said George. 'But one of the men had left his coat in the back of the car and there was a notebook with a pencil in the breast-pocket. I just used that!'

'Jolly good!' said Julian.

'Well, they whizzed me off in the car to some fair-ground or other,' said George. 'I heard the roundabout music next day. There was a horrid old witch-like woman in the caravan; she didn't seem at all pleased to see me. I had to sleep in a chair that night, and I got so wild that I yelled and shouted and threw things about and smashed quite a lot of cups and saucers. I enjoyed that.'

The boys couldn't help laughing. 'Yes – I bet you did,' said Dick. 'They had to move the caravan away from the fair itself, because they were afraid people would hear you. In fact, I expect that's why Gringo decided to hide you here!'

'Yes. I suddenly felt a jolt, and found the caravan we were in was being towed away!' said George. 'I was awfully surprised. I waved at the windows and shouted as we drove through the streets, but nobody seemed to notice anything wrong – in fact some people waved back to me! Then we swung in through some gates, and came here – and, as I told you, they put me up here because I made such a nuisance of myself!'

'Did you tell them you weren't Berta?' asked Dick.

'No,' said George. 'Of course not. For two reasons – I knew there would be no fear of Berta's father giving those secrets away, because he'd be told by you that *I* had been kidnapped, not his precious Berta. So he'd hang on to them. And also I thought *Berta* would be safe, so long as I didn't tell the men they'd got the wrong person.'

'You're a good kid, George,' said Julian, and

slapped her gently on the back. 'A – very – good – kid.
I'm jolly proud of you. There's nobody like our
George!'

'Don't be an idiot,' said George, but she was very
pleased all the same.

'Well, there's no more to tell,' she said, 'except that
the cistern room was most frightfully draughty, and I
had to wrap my head up as well as my body when I lay
down. And the cistern made awful noises – sort of *rude*
noises, that made me want to say "I beg your par-
don!"all the time! Of course I knew you'd rescue me,
so I wasn't awfully worried!'

'And we *haven't* rescued you!' said Julian. 'All we've
done is to get ourselves locked up as well as you!'

'Tell me how you found out I was here,' said
George. So the boys told her everything and she
listened, thrilled.

'So Berta went to stay with Jo!' she said. 'I bet Jo
didn't like that.'

'She didn't,' said Julian. 'But she's been quite a help.
I only wish she were here now, and could do one of her
ivy-climbing stunts, or something!'

'I say – Timmy's very quiet all of a sudden!' said
George, listening. 'What's happened?'

They listened. Timmy was not barking or whimpering. There was no sound from him at all. What was
happening? George's heart sank – perhaps those men
had managed to do something to him?

But suddenly they heard him again, whimpering –
but whimpering gladly and excitedly. And then a
familiar voice came to their ears.

'Dick! Julian! Where are you?'

'Gosh – it's JO!' said Dick, astounded. He limped to
the door. 'We're in here, Jo. Unlock the door!'

Jo unlocked it and looked in, grinning. Timmy tore
in like a whirlwind and flung himself on George,

almost knocking her over. Dick limped out of the room immediately Jo rushed in, much to everyone's astonishment. Then he returned, looking rather pleased with himself.

'Let's go while the going's good,' he said.

'Yes – but, be careful, those men will be out, now that Timmy isn't there to guard them!' cried Julian, suddenly realising that the two angry fellows could easily escape while Timmy was in with them – and might lock the door on the lot of them, Timmy too!

'It's all right – there's no desperate hurry!' said Dick. 'I thought of that. I slipped out and locked their door on *them*, as soon as Jo rushed in to us. And there they can stay till the police arrive in the morning. They can then collect the whole lot – the men upstairs too.'

'And I'm sure the police will be quite pleased to search the house and the cellars,' said Julian. 'There will be plenty of stuff here that they will be interested in! Well, let's go at once.'

They called a cheery goodbye to the two men. 'We're off!' shouted Dick. 'You'd better look out for the dog in case he gets you!' They all went down the hall, Dick hobbling, for his ankle was still painful.

'We might as well leave in style,' said Julian, and unbolted and unlocked the front door. 'Also it would be as well to leave this door open for the police to come in by – I don't expect *they* will want to come in through the coal-hole! It was a good idea of yours to let the men think we were leaving Tim behind to guard them, Dick – they won't dare even to climb out of the windows in case he's waiting for them!'

'We've left a good many lights on,' said George, looking back. 'Never mind – we're not paying the bill! Come on, Timmy, out into the dark, dark night!'

They went down the front steps and into the dark drive. Everyone felt safe with Timmy running ahead.

'Jo — exactly how did you get here?' said Dick, suddenly. 'You were forbidden to come.'

'I know,' said Jo. 'Well, I just took Anne's bike and followed you, that's all. And I walked in through the front gates when you'd left them open, of course. That was easy.'

'Gosh — I kept *feeling* there was someone behind me!' said Dick. 'And there was — it was *you*, you little horror! No wonder Timmy didn't bother to bark or growl.'

'Yes, it was me,' said Jo. 'And I followed you round and round the house, while you were trying to get in — and I thought you never *would* see that coal-hole — so I took the lid off and put it on the ground, hoping you'd see it then. And you did!'

'So *you* did that!' said Dick. 'I must say I was astonished to see it. I knew we must have passed it before. So that was you too! You want a good telling off, you disobedient, cheeky little wretch!'

Jo laughed. 'I couldn't bear you to go off without me,' she said. 'It's a good thing I *did* come! I waited and waited inside that coal-hole for you to come back with George — and when you didn't, I left the coal-hole and got into the house. And Timmy heard me and came running down the stairs. He nearly knocked me over, he was that pleased!'

'Here are the gates at last,' said George. 'What are we going to do about bikes? There isn't one for me.'

'Jo can stand behind on my step and hold on to my shoulder,' said Julian. 'You take Anne's bike, George. We'll leave these gates open. The police ought to be pleased with us for saving them so much trouble!'

Off they went down the steep hill, Timmy running behind, his tail wagging happily. He had got George back again. All was well again in his doggy world!

22 'These kids sure are wunnerful!'

What shrieks and shouts there were from Joanna and Anne when the four arrived at Kirrin Cottage at last, at half past three in the morning! Joanna was awake, but Anne had just gone to sleep. She was sleeping in Joanna's room for company and Sally was there too.

The stories had to be told again and again. First Dick, then Julian, then George, then Jo – they all talked without stopping, excited and happy. Sally ran from one to the other, and followed Timmy about – but sometimes her little stiff tail drooped when she remembered that Berta was not there.

'I *say*,' said Dick, suddenly drawing back the sitting-room curtains '– it's daylight! The sun's up! And all the time I've been thinking it was still night!'

'No use going to bed, then,' said Jo, at once. She was so much enjoying this that she felt as if she never wanted it to stop!

'Well, I suppose it isn't,' said Joanna. 'I know what we'll do – we'll have a big breakfast now, a very big one to celebrate – and then we'll all go back to bed and sleep till lunch-time. We're tired out really – just look at our black-rimmed eyes and pale cheeks!'

'Joanna! We're all as sunburnt as can be, you're just making that up!' said George. 'Come on – let's get this celebration breakfast going! Bacon – eggs – tomatoes – fried bread. Oh, and mushrooms too – have you any mushrooms, Joanna? And lots and lots of hot coffee, and toast and marmalade. I'm ravenous.'

They discovered that they all were, and twenty minues later they sat at the table tucking in as if they had eaten nothing for a month.

'I can't eat a thing more,' said Dick, 'and I don't know what's happened to my eyes – they keep closing!'

'So do mine,' said George, with an enormous yawn. 'Joanna – don't say we've got to do the washing-up, will you?'

'Of course not!' said Joanna. 'Go on up to your beds now – don't even bother to undress.'

'I feel as if there's something I ought to do – but I can't remember it,' said Julian, sleepily, staggering upstairs. 'I – just – can't remember!'

He flopped on his bed and was asleep as soon as his head fell on the pillow. In two minutes everyone but Joanna was asleep too. Joanna stopped to give Timmy a drink, and then he bounded up to George and curled up in the crook of her knees as usual.

Joanna went to lie down too, thinking she would just have a rest, but not go to sleep. But in half a second she slept too.

The sun rose higher in the sky. The milkman came whistling up the path and left four bottles of milk on the step. The gulls in the bay circled and soared and called loudly. But nobody stirred in Kirrin Cottage.

A car came up to the front gate, and another one followed. Out of the first stepped Uncle Quentin, Aunt Fanny, Mr Elbur Wright – and Berta! Out of the second car stepped the sergeant and his constable.

Berta flew to the front door, but it was shut. She raced round to the garden door. That was locked too – and so was the kitchen door!

'Pops! We'll have to ring – all the doors are locked!'

she called. And then, from up above came a sound of excited barking, and Sally's head appeared at a bedroom window. When she saw it really was Berta down below, she tore down the stairs and scraped at the front door.

'What's happened? Where *is* everyone?' said Aunt Fanny in amazement. '*All* the doors locked? But it's ten o'clock in the morning. Where are the children?'

'I've got my key,' said Uncle Quentin, and he put it into the front door lock. He opened the door and Sally leapt straight into Berta's arms, licking her face from forehead to chin!

Aunt Fanny went into the hall and called, 'Anyone at home?'

No answer. Timmy heard her call, but as George did not stir, he didn't either. He was not going to leave George for a minute, not even to go downstairs!

Aunt Fanny walked into all the rooms on the ground floor. Nobody there! She marvelled at the remains of the meal spread all over the dining-room table, and even more at the dirty pans and dishes in the kitchen. What was Joanna thinking of? WHERE was everybody? She did not expect George to be there, because she knew George had been kidnapped – but where in the world were all the others?

She went upstairs and her husband followed with Berta and her father. They were all feeling most astonished now. They went into Julian's room – good gracious he *was* there, then! And Dick too – lying floppily on their beds, absolutely sound asleep! Aunt Fanny couldn't understand it.

And then she went into the girls' room – and there was Anne fast asleep too – and GOOD GRACIOUS, could that be *George*? But surely George was kidnapped – then how – why – where . . .

Her mother suddenly put her arms round the

sleeping George and kissed her and hugged her. She had worried so much about her – and now here she was, safe and sound after all!

George awoke at once. She sat up and gazed at her mother and father in atonishment.

'Oh – you're back! Oh, how lovely! When did you come?'

'Just now,' said her mother. 'But George – why is everyone asleep – and how did *you* get here – we thought you were . . .'

'Oh, Mother – yes, of course you don't know half the story, do you?' said George. 'Gosh, there's Berta here too – and your pops, Berta! Hallo, everyone.'

She was still so sleepy that she was not quite sure whether this was a dream or not. But then Anne woke up and squealed, and that woke Julian and Dick. They came into the very crowded bedroom, and soon there was such a noise that Joanna and Jo, in the room above, awoke too.

Down they came, looking very dishevelled, Joanna full of apologies. She rushed downstairs to put some coffee on and bumped into the two policemen in the hall. She screamed.

'Excuse me,' said the sergeant to Joanna. 'Isn't anyone ever coming down again? We're supposed to be guarding Berta.'

'Oh my – you don't need to do that now!' said Joanna. 'Didn't Julian telephone you last night – this morning, I mean – I thought he was going to.'

'What about?' said the sergeant.

'About the kidnappers. Everything's all right,' explained Joanna to the two astonished policemen. 'We've got George back – and oh, bless us all, there's those kidnappers – you haven't been told they're all locked up and waiting for you, have you?'

'Look here, what *are* you talking about?' said the

sergeant, bewildered. 'This is too bad – what do you *mean* – kidnappers locked up and waiting!'

'Julian! called Joanna, 'The police are here – and you forgot to telephone and tell them what happened last night. They'd better go to that house and get the men, hadn't they?'

'I *knew* there was something I'd forgotten,' said Julian, running down the stairs. 'I did mean to telephone, but I was so tired that I forgot.'

Everyone then came downstairs and went into the sitting-room. Jo was shy with so many people there, and wouldn't sit anywhere near the two policemen.

'I've just been told, Mr Wright, that there's no need to guard your daughter now,' said the sergeant, rather stiffly. 'Seems as if the police are the last to hear about anything!'

'Well, the fact of the matter is that we found out that Gringo, who owns the fair called Gringo's Fair, was paid to kidnap Berta,' said Julian. 'He kidnapped George instead, by mistake. We found out where Gringo had taken her and went to rescue her last night. You go on, Dick.'

'And we left Gringo and somebody else locked up in a room on the ground floor, and two other people locked up in a top-floor room – and we've left the front door open for you and the drive gates open too,' said Dick. 'So don't be too annoyed about it, Sergeant, because we really have tried to make things easy for you! We've rescued George, as you see – and now *you* can get the men.'

The sergeant looked as if he found it difficult to believe a single word! Uncle Quentin tapped him sharply on the shoulder.

'Well, look alive, man – they'll escape before you can get them if you don't hurry.'

'What's the address?' said the sergeant, stolidly.

'I don't know the name of the house, or the lane it's in,' said Julian. 'But you go through the village of Twining, turn to the left, and it's the house up on the hill.'

'How did you find out all this?' said the sergeant.

'It's too long to tell you now!' said Dick. 'We'll write it all down in a book, and send you a copy. We'll call it – er – we'll call it – what *shall* we call it, you others? It's a peculiar adventure really – it ended with everyone fast asleep in bed!'

'I want some coffee,' announced Uncle Quentin. 'I think we've talked enough. Do go and catch your kidnappers, my good men.'

The policemen disappeared. Mr Elbur Wright beamed round happily, Berta on his knee.

'Well, this is a very happy ending!' he said. 'And I can take my little Berta back with me after all!'

'Oh no!' wailed Berta, much to her father's surprise.

'What do you mean?' he asked.

'Gee, Pops, be a honey and let me stay on here,' begged Berta. 'These kids sure are wunnerful.'

'WonDERful, wonDERful, wonDERful!' chanted the others.

'Of course let her stay on if she'd like to,' said Aunt Fanny. 'But as a girl this time, not as a boy!'

George heaved a sigh of relief. That was all right then. She wouldn't mind Berta as a girl, even though she was a *silly* girl!

'Woof!' said Timmy suddenly, and made everyone jump.

'He says he's jolly pleased you're staying, Berta, because now Sally-dog will have to stay too,' said Dick. 'So *he'll* have someone to play with as well!'

'Shall we really send the sergeant a book about this adventure?' said Anne. 'Did you *really* mean it, Dick?'

'Rather!' said Dick. 'Our fourteenth adventure –

and may we have many more! What shall we call the book?'

'I know!' said George, at once. 'I know! Let's call it "FIVE HAVE PLENTY OF FUN".'

Well, they did – and they hope you like it!

The Enid Blyton Newsletter

Would you like to receive The Enid Blyton Newsletter? It has lots of news about Enid Blyton books, videos, plays, etc. There are also puzzles and a page for your letters. It is published three times a year and is free for children who live in the United Kingdom and Ireland.

If you would like to receive it for a year, please write to: The Enid Blyton Newsletter, PO Box 357, London, WC2N 6QB, sending your name and address. (UK and Ireland only)